THE

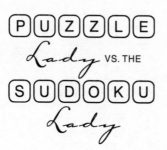

PUZZLE
Lady VS. THE
SUDOKU
Lady

Also by Parnell Hall

THE

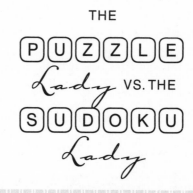

A Puzzle Lady Mystery

Parnell Hall

MINOTAUR BOOKS
A THOMAS DUNNE BOOK
New York

This is a work of fiction. All of the characters, organizations, and events portrayed in this novel are either products of the author's imagination or are used fictitiously.

A THOMAS DUNNE BOOK FOR MINOTAUR BOOKS.
An imprint of St. Martin's Publishing Group.

www.thomasdunnebooks.com
www.minotaurbooks.com

Library of Congress Cataloging-in-Publication Data

Hall, Parnell.
   The Puzzle Lady vs. The Sudoku Lady : a Puzzle Lady mystery / Parnell
Hall. — 1st ed.
      p.   cm.
   "A Thomas Dunne book for Minotaur Books"—T. p. verso.
   ISBN 978-0-312-61218-4
   1. Felton, Cora (Fictitious character)—Fiction.   2. Crossword
puzzle makers—Fiction.   3. Women—Crimes against—Fiction.
4. Sudoku—Fiction.   I. Title.
   PS3558.A37327P79 2010
   813'.54—dc22

                                                        2009034525

10 9 8 7 6 5 4 3 2

For Ruth,
who suggested The Sudoku Lady

The Perpetrators

I would like to thank Will Shortz, *New York Times* crossword puzzle editor and NPR puzzlemaster, for constructing all the sudoku that appear in this book. I didn't tell him they would be used for blackmail. I hope he doesn't mind.

I would like to thank frequent *New York Times* contributor Manny Nosowsky for constructing the blackmail notes. Manny proved surprisingly adept at extortion. I will have to watch him in the future.

I would like to thank National Champion Ellen Ripstein for editing the puzzles. She didn't know they were blackmail notes. Or so she says. I'd watch her, too.

Last, but not least, I would like to thank the incomparable Ruth Cavin for the Sudoku Lady. The Puzzle Lady meeting her Japanese counterpart was Ruth's idea.

Clearly she bears watching.

THE

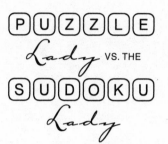

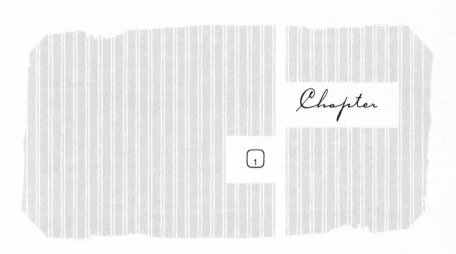

Chapter

1

"You don't have to go."

"Oh, yes I do," Cora said. "You're young, you're in love, you just got married. You're setting up your home. You don't need some spinster aunt in the spare room cramping your style."

Sherry smiled. "I don't think a woman who's been married five or six times qualifies as a spinster."

"I don't care what you call me, the fact is I'm a drag. I gotta get out of here."

"Cora. Aaron's been living here the last six months. Nothing's changed just because we said 'I do.'"

"Are you kidding me? *Everything* changes when you say 'I do.' You stop making allowances, treating each other nice, ignoring each other's faults, forgiving each other's sins. Good lord, girl, what's the point of getting him hooked if you're not going to reel him in?"

Sherry smiled. "You're not that cynical. You're talking tough right now because you're not in love. Just let a handsome man come around, you'll melt like butter."

After a long courtship, Sherry Carter had finally tied the knot with young reporter Aaron Grant. The newlyweds were back from their honeymoon, and Cora Felton had brought up her avowed intention of moving out. The prefab ranch house Cora shared with her niece in Bakerhaven, Connecticut, was small, to say the least, particularly since they'd converted the third bedroom into an office.

"You haven't thought this through."

Cora winced. "I hate that expression. It's a euphemism for 'You're a dotty old lady with the brains of a tree stump.'"

"That isn't what I said."

"Of course, it isn't. That's what *euphemism* means. I don't have to tell you. You're the wordsmith."

Which she was. Sherry Carter was a brilliant crossword puzzle constructor, whose puzzles appeared daily in a nationally syndicated column. Only no one knew it. At the time Sherry came up with the idea, she was keeping a low profile on account of her obsessive and abusive ex-husband. So she put her aunt's name on the column. Which worked like a charm. No one observing Cora Felton's benign, grandmotherly face, with twinkling eyes and beatific smile, could ever suspect that the amiable fraud couldn't solve a crossword puzzle with a gun to her head.

"You're the Puzzle Lady. When people ask you to solve a puzzle, what are you going to tell them?"

"I'm on vacation."

"Permanent vacation? Are you never going to solve a puzzle again?"

"Works for me."

"What if someone brings you a crossword puzzle involved in a crime?"

"Don't be silly."

"Why is that silly?"

"That isn't going to happen."

"It happens all the time. You can't turn around without someone knocking on the door wanting you to solve a puzzle found at the scene of a murder."

Cora smiled, spread her hands. "Exactly. I have used up my quota. The law of averages says it won't happen again."

"The law of averages doesn't apply."

"No?"

"Of course not. We're flipping a coin. Each time we flip it, it's as likely to come up heads as it is tails. Isn't that right?"

"Of course."

"Even if it's come up heads ten times in a row?"

"Huh?"

"Say I flip a coin. It comes up heads ten times in a row. Now I flip it again. Is it more likely to come up heads or tails?"

"Sherry, you're my niece and I love you. But if you torture me with logic, I'm going to tie that supple body of yours in a knot."

"You're good at logic."

"Human logic. Practical puzzles. Not this theoretical crap."

"The point is, you can't function without me."

"Give me a break. You went off on your honeymoon; I did just fine."

"You text-messaged me in Africa. You sent me a puzzle as an attached file."

"Aren't you proud of me for knowing how to do that?"

"I left you instructions a child could follow."

"Exactly. Kids are much better at computers than grown-ups. I think I did remarkably well."

"I give up. If you want to leave, I can't stop you. But, please, don't think Aaron and I are driving you away."

The kitchen phone rang.

Sherry scooped the receiver off the wall. "Hello?" Her face hardened. "You have to stop calling," she said, and hung up.

"Dennis?" Cora asked.

Sherry frowned. "I'm going to have to get caller ID."

"That guy is seriously sick."

"I'd hoped my getting married would give him a hint. It seems to have just ticked him off."

"Good thing you've got a restraining order."

"Yeah, like that's going to stop him. Particularly when he's drunk. It's not good. Aaron's gone all day. I'm helpless here."

"I could teach you how to shoot."

"I don't want to shoot him. I just want to be left alone."

"That's why I'm moving out."

The phone rang again.

Sherry looked at it in exasperation.

"I've got it this time," Cora said. She snatched the phone off the hook and snarled "Yes."

A rather disconcerted voice on the other end said, "Cora Felton?"

Cora rolled her eyes for her niece's benefit, said, "This is she."

"The Puzzle Lady?"

Cora managed not to groan. "That's right."

"This is your agent. Sebastian Billingham."

Cora reacted as if the phone were hot. Her agent was, of course, Sherry's agent. He handled the Puzzle Lady books Sherry pub-
under Cora's name. Next to Dennis, Cora couldn't think of

a person she cared less to talk to. Including Dennis, actually. Cora would get a kick out of bawling out Dennis.

"Oh, yes, Mr. Billingham. You want to talk to my personal assistant, Sherry Carter. She handles all my business affairs."

Cora tossed the phone to Sherry and skipped out of reach before Sherry could hand it back.

Sherry looked at her aunt in exasperation, placed the phone to her ear. "This is Sherry Carter. How may I help you? . . . Uh huh . . . Uh huh . . . That's good."

Cora beamed.

Sherry frowned. "That's *not* good? Why is that not good?"

Cora shot Sherry a glance as if to say, *Can't you do anything right?*

"Uh huh . . . Uh huh . . . Uh huh," Sherry said.

Cora found this less than illuminating. She spread her arms, made a face like *Huh?*

"Today?" Sherry said. "Well, you might have given us a little notice . . . What do you mean, you just found out? . . . I understand you're not her agent."

Cora's mouth fell open. She tugged at Sherry's shirt, hissed, "What do you mean, he's not my agent?"

Sherry batted her hands away. "Trust me, you *don't* want to tell her yourself."

"Tell me *what*?" Cora demanded.

"Thank you very much. Okay. Good-bye."

Sherry hung up the phone and turned to face her aunt.

Cora cocked her head. "What do you call it when you kill your niece? I know it's matricide when you kill your mother. For that matter, what do you call it when you kill your agent?"

"It's not his fault. He just found out and called to warn us."

"About what?"

"Minami is coming."

"Who?"

"Minami."

"Who the hell is that?"

"The Sudoku Lady."

Chapter

2

Cora sucked on a cigarette as if she needed every last gram of nicotine. She blew smoke out of her nose and mouth. It was a wonder it wasn't coming out of her ears.

"So, some woman I never met, laid eyes on, or even heard of, is challenging me to a duel?"

"Not exactly."

"*How* not exactly?"

"Okay. Here's the situation. You have the number-one best-selling sudoku book in Japan. Which is great, except Minami has the number-*two* best-selling sudoku book in Japan. Last week she was number one. And the week before that. And the week before that. And the week before that. A foreigner comes along and knocks her book down to number two."

"I'd like to knock *her* down to number two."

"Cora."

"Go on."

"According to Sebastian Billingham—"

"Who?"

"Your agent."

"Oh."

"According to him, you brought shame and dishonor on her and all her family, and she cannot rest until she's been avenged."

"You're kidding!"

"Yes, I am. The woman is not really challenging you to sudoku at forty paces."

"Too bad. I bet I could take her."

Cora was surprisingly good at sudoku. She was a klutz at word problems, but at number problems she was a whiz.

"You don't have to take her. You just have to sit down and be civil."

"Why?"

"Am I a mind reader? You want me to psychoanalyze, sight unseen, the motivations of a Japanese sudoku constructor?"

There came the sound of tires in the driveway.

"Oh, my God, she's here! Cora, you're not dressed!"

"What do you mean I'm not dressed?"

Cora was wearing her Wicked Witch of the West outfit, a loose-fitting smock with food stains and cigarette burns and dangling threads and small tears.

"You can't meet her like that. I'll stall her. You go change."

"I'm not kowtowing to any Japanese diva."

"Wrong attitude! For any number of reasons." Sherry herded her aunt out of the kitchen. "Just throw something on."

Muttering to herself, Cora padded down the hall to her bedroom, pulled the Wicked Witch of the West smock up over her head. She was *not* dressing up for the woman. Her standard Miss Marplewear, a tweed skirt and jacket, would do perfectly well.

Even if the skirt was a little tight. Which was why Cora was wearing the free-flowing smock. Was it time to start dieting again? Not without a man in the picture. What was the point? Sweets were no substitute for a suitor, but the thought of doing without either was more than one could bear.

Cora snapped her skirt, pulled on the matching tweed jacket. She could hear Sherry opening the front door. Cora steeled herself, went out to meet her visitor.

It was Chief Harper.

The Bakerhaven chief of police was obviously ill at ease. Which was odd, since he and Cora Felton had worked together often enough to have developed an ongoing comaraderie, if not a mutual respect. Cora hadn't seen him this uncomfortable since the time he'd had to arrest her for murder.

"Hi, Chief. What's up?"

"Hi, Cora."

"Well, don't stand in the doorway. Sherry, aren't you going to ask him in?"

"I can't stay," Harper said. "There's been a murder."

"Really?" Cora's interest perked up immediately.

"Yeah. Mrs. Fielding, out on Kingston Road."

"Ida?"

"You know her?"

"It's a small town, Chief. I don't know her well, but I've seen her in the bakeshop. If it's the same one I'm thinking of."

"Little woman, curly hair."

"That's her. How'd she die?"

"Fell in a fireplace, banged her head on an andiron."

"And that's murder?"

"It would seem to be accidental. But a few things don't add up."

"Such as?"

"If she fell on an andiron, why did it bash in the top of her head? I don't mean the top of her head; I mean the side that was up."

"She couldn't have bounced?"

"Bounced? On an andiron?"

"You know what I mean. She fell on an andiron, rolled off, lay on her side, and expired."

"I suppose she could have. And probably did."

"Come on, Chief, what makes you think this was a crime?"

"Well . . ."

"Is there a crossword puzzle involved?"

"No."

"A sudoku?"

"No."

"An acrostic? A cryptogram? Anything like that?"

"No. No puzzle at all. She probably just fell. But I can't help thinking, what if it's murder?"

"Ten to one it's a domestic thing. Why don't you lock up her husband?"

"I did."

"So?"

Harper grimaced. "Unfortunately, I locked him up the night

before. Drunk and disorderly. Bar fight down at Benny's. He was in jail all night."

Cora nodded. "Which he would naturally do if he was giving himself an alibi. The minute he realized he'd killed her, he went out and got in a bar fight and got thrown in jail."

"Not according to Barney Nathan. His preliminary estimate of the time of death is between eleven o'clock and two A.M. We locked hubby up around ten forty-five."

"That doesn't sound very promising."

"No, it doesn't." Harper scratched his head. He seemed to be trying to think of what to say next.

Cora smiled. "Tell me, Chief, if there's no puzzle involved, why are you here?"

"Oh."

"You have some ulterior motive, don't you? You've been acting like a shoplifter ever since you came in the door."

"Shoplifter?"

"Spill it."

Chief Harper exhaled. "Oh, for God's sake, I'm the chief of police. It's my job to solve crimes. It's your job to write crossword puzzles."

Cora didn't correct the chief on that point. "So?"

"This crime doesn't have one. There's absolutely no reason for me to be here. If anyone knew I was talking to you about this case, they'd want to know why."

"Why *are* you talking to me about this case?"

"Because you're good at it. That's what I don't get. Why are people so quick to dismiss your theories when you're right so much of the time?"

"I've wondered that myself."

"Let's not go overboard. The fact is, you're intuitive and per-ceptive when it comes to analyzing clues."

"Careful, Chief, I'll get a swelled head."

"Anyway, the husband's still in jail, and the body's in the morgue."

Cora squinted at him. "You want me to take a look at the scene of the crime?"

"If you wouldn't mind."

"Thought you'd never ask."

Chapter

4

Michiko piloted the car around the curve, tugged at her sleeve. "I hate this damn kimono."

Minami stuck her chin in the air, looked across at her niece. "Do not say 'damn.'"

"It is more polite than some things I might say. Why did you bring me here?"

"You know why."

"I know why we travel together. I do not know why we are here."

"I must see this woman for myself," Minami said.

"Why? Why does it matter? She has a sudoku book. You have a sudoku book. You have many sudoku books."

"What if she writes another?"

"Then you are ready," Michiko said, impatiently. She pouted. "Why can't we go to the mall?"

"We went to the mall."

"But you did not let me buy the pants."

"Those pants had no front."

"What?"

"And no back."

"That is the style."

"The waist was around your ankles. It is not decent."

"That is what the girls are wearing."

"That is not what the girls are wearing. That is what the boys *wish* the girls were wearing."

"Don't you want the boys to like me?"

"You are only sixteen."

"I am going to be seventeen."

"Your birthday was last month."

"And what did I get? A silk kimono!"

"You look very good."

"I look like a silkscreen painting. I want to look like a girl."

"We come in peace and friendship."

"Yeah, right."

"'Yeah, right'? That sounds rude. Is that American? 'Yeah, right'?"

"Yeah, right."

"Michiko." Minami shook her head. It was a hopeless task, trying to explain to a teenager who wouldn't listen. "This Puzzle Lady, she is a big deal. Her TV ads play in our country."

"*Your* TV ads play in our country."

"I *live* in our country. My TV ads do not play in the United States."

"They're in Japanese."

"That is not the point."

"Yeah, yeah, that is not the point. I do not know what the point is, but it is not that."

"Are you being rude again?"

"No."

"It is important that I do well here."

"That is stupid."

"It is not stupid. It is a matter of honor."

"Oh, pooh."

"Do not pooh honor." Minami shook her head. "You are young—you do not know."

"Yes, yes, I am young—I do not know," Michiko mimicked. "That is what you always say. Ever since I was ten. I am not ten anymore."

"No, but you act like it."

"I will stop the car."

"You will not stop the car. You will drive the car, and I will keep my appointment. And my books will sell many copies and you will go to the best school where you will learn many things."

"I can't wait."

"Maybe you will even learn manners."

A police car whizzed by, heading in the opposite direction.

Minami's eyes widened. "Stop the car!"

"What?"

"Stop the car!"

"You said don't stop the car."

"Stop the car! Turn around!"

"Why?"

"That was her!"

Chapter

5

Chief Harper glanced over at Cora in the passenger seat. "So, what are you so eager to get away from?"

"Huh?"

"You ran out of there like the house was on fire. What's up?"

"Are you kidding? You got a murder case."

"Well, it's not the crime of the century. If it's even a crime. By your standards, it's pretty dull."

"That's a hell of an attitude, Chief. After all, Ida's dead."

"Are you sure her name is Ida?"

"How long have you lived in this town? A lot longer than I have, that's for sure. You oughta know everyone."

"I knew her by sight."

"How'd you know her last name?"

"Doctor told me. And it was on the mailbox. And she's Jason's wife."

"How come you know his name and not hers?"

"I never arrested her."

"If her husband's in jail, who found her?"

"Cleaning lady."

"She had a cleaning lady?"

"What's wrong with that?"

"I don't have a cleaning lady."

"You live with your niece."

"Oh."

"What?"

"I gotta move out."

"Why?"

"Why? She's a newlywed. You know what that's like. Well, you probably don't remember."

Harper flushed slightly, said, "You changed the subject nicely."

"From what?"

"Why were you so eager to get out of the house?"

"Oh. I got company coming."

"What?"

Cora told Chief Harper about the Sudoku Lady.

"There's a Japanese puzzle constructor showing up at your house?"

"That's the rumor."

"You haven't spoken to her?"

"I don't know her."

"How come she hasn't called?"

"She doesn't know me."

Chief Harper shook his head. "Last time we had Japanese visitors it didn't turn out so well."

"I got a book contract."

"And people wound up dead."

"That was an added bonus."

Chief Harper pulled into the driveway of a two-story frame house, white, with green shutters, like half the other homes in town.

"Distinctive," Cora said.

The door was locked. Chief Harper produced a key.

"Where did you get that?"

"Cleaning lady."

They went through the foyer into the living room.

Ashes, spilled out from the hearth, marked where the body had lain.

"Which andiron?" Cora said.

"The one on the right."

Cora bent down, reached into her floppy, drawstring purse. She pulled out a handkerchief, moved the andiron slightly. "Heavy. No one picked this up and bopped her on the head."

"Right."

"A trace of blood on the edge?"

"Yes, it is. It's not conclusive."

"That's not what I mean. If it's her blood, which is entirely likely, the evidence would indicate she fell on the andiron."

"Yes."

"And bounced off and rolled over and expired."

"I suppose," Harper said grudgingly.

"What's wrong with that?"

"The wound wasn't very deep. I've seen a guy with a tenpenny spike in his head." Cora looked at him in amazement. He waved his hand. "Nail gun accident. Never mind. The point is, that guy lived. This was a shallow cut."

"What does Barney say?"

"Says she's dead. Which I could have figured. As to why, he said that might take longer. From which I gather, our medical examiner has an early tee time. That's golf, not tea and crumpets."

"Crumpets? Chief, are you sure you're not British?"

"The thing is, we don't have a cause of death except for the blow on the head. If we assume the andiron didn't kill her, the question is why did she fall in the hearth."

"If she was backing up from an intruder, she could have tripped over the coffee table."

Harper frowned. "Would that be murder?"

Cora studied the coffee table, considering the idea. "If she was backing away from an intruder, I would say any harm she encountered would be a direct result of the menacing act. How's that work for you, Chief? Could a person trip over the coffee table and fall in the grate?"

"I don't know. But I don't have to. Look where the table is. You'd have to take two steps sideways to hit the andiron."

"Unless you were flung with force."

"Are you saying she was pushed over backward?"

"Isn't that better for all concerned? Well, not for Ida, of course. She hadn't been drinking?"

"Again, we have to wait for Barney Nathan. But she hadn't apparently been drinking. So, any ideas?"

"I like the husband."

"The one that's in jail with the perfect alibi."

"That's why I like him. If you were going to kill your wife, you'd of course have a perfect alibi."

"If it's perfect, he couldn't have done it."

"He made it *appear* perfect. We just have to figure out how."

Chief Harper groaned. "Please don't tell me you're going to

come up with another one of your convoluted—" He broke off at a sound from the foyer.

"Was that the front door?" Cora said.

"It couldn't be. Jason's still in jail."

Chief Harper turned and gawked.

Standing in the doorway were an attractive Japanese woman, in a few hundred yards of ornate silk, and a rather sullen-looking Japanese teenager.

The woman fluttered her arms like an immense silken butterfly, smiled brightly, and said, "Hello."

Chapter

6

The Japanese woman could not have seemed more comfortable had she been in her own living room. "Forgive me," she said. "We have not officially met. I am Minami, the Sudoku Lady. This is my niece, Michiko. And you are the famous Puzzle Lady."

Cora stared at her. "What in the world are you doing here?"

"I am on my way to your house when I see you in a police car. I think you may need help."

"You thought I'd been arrested?"

"I do not know what to think. Your American customs are not the same as ours. Perhaps you use police cars the way we use taxis."

"Forgive me for interrupting, but I am the chief of police. I still don't know what you're doing here."

"If you are the chief of police, it is a piece of good luck. Perhaps there is a crime."

"Why would that be a bit of good luck?"

"I like crime. I am sorry, that is not to say I like it, but when it has happened, I like to figure it out. It is like solving a puzzle."

"It is *not* like solving a puzzle," Chief Harper said. "When you solve a puzzle, no one is dead."

"Someone is dead? This is a crime scene?"

"Yes."

"Then why is there no ribbon? On American television, when there is a crime scene, there is a ribbon. Or is that just on TV?"

"No, we use crime scene ribbons."

"But you do not have one. So you are not sure it is a crime."

"The woman fell and hit her head in the fireplace. She died."

Minami nodded sagely. "You should arrest her husband."

Harper's mouth fell open. "Why do you say that?"

"When a wife is killed, it is most often the husband." Minami indicated Cora. "Has she not told you this? You have the big reputation for solving crime."

"Do I now?"

"In our country. It is why they buy your book."

Cora Felton dug her hand into her drawstring purse. Harper wondered if she was going for her gun. Instead, she came out with her cigarettes. She pulled one out, put it in her mouth. On second thought, she offered one to Minami.

"I do not smoke."

"I'll have one," Michiko said.

"You will not! Your parents did not let you go with me to learn bad habits." Minami raised a disapproving eyebrow at Cora. "I am surprised you would be such a bad example. You are supposed to be a role model."

"Yeah, right," Cora said, and lit her cigarette.

"See? *She* says it," Michiko said.

"This is getting out of hand," Harper said. "Let's take it outside, put up a crime scene ribbon."

"You will arrest the husband?"

"I already arrested the husband."

Her eyes widened. "I do not understand. You are not sure it is a murder, and yet you have made an arrest."

"I arrested the husband for being drunk and disorderly. I arrested him *last night*. He was in jail when she was killed. That's why there is no crime scene ribbon. It was probably an accidental death."

"Are you sure he did not plan to be arrested? Kill her and then go to jail?"

"I think it's pretty clear that did not happen. As soon as I can confirm it, I'll let him go."

The Sudoku Lady turned to Cora. "You are busy. Our meeting must be postponed. My niece and I must find a place to stay. We will contact you when this unfortunate incident is behind us."

Minami backed away, bowing and smiling, and herding her young niece toward the car.

Chapter

7

Chief Harper glanced over at Cora. They were halfway back to town, and the Puzzle Lady hadn't said a word. "Penny for your thoughts."

"Take a wild guess."

"You're not happy with our new acquaintance?"

"Well, isn't she the most annoying woman?"

"I've met some pretty annoying women."

"Give me a break. She just wanders into the crime scene and starts poking around."

"There was no crime scene ribbon."

"Now you're taking her side?"

"Side? You both have sudoku books. What, it's like who has the best numbers? I thought you only used one through nine."

"Go ahead, make fun. Here the woman just waltzes in without so much as a howdy-do and starts poking into the case."

"You find that irritating? I'd be interested to get your opinion on that."

Cora gave him a look. "Is that irony? Are you trying to use irony on me, Chief? You're not that good at it. You really need symbols. Like on the Internet. Emoticons, so people will know you're kidding. I hate that. Kind of ruins a deadpan, you know what I mean?"

"What are you talking about?"

"Nothing. I'm just talking. Tell me, do you think this is an accidental death?"

"Of course it is."

"Then why did we just spend forty-five minutes poking around the hearth examining every little thing?"

"I like to be sure."

"You were pretty sure before Little Miss Sudoku stuck her nose in."

"I still am."

"So, what changed?"

"If somebody's going to make a fuss, I like to be prepared. If there are questions, I like to have answers."

"Did you get any?"

"There's none to get. You know it, and I know it. There's nothing left to do but offer Jason our sympathy and let him out of jail."

"I wish our Japanese friend could be there. Not that I want to rub it in her face, you understand."

Chief Harper pulled up in front of the police station, a white frame building distinguishable from the others on the block only by a black-and-white wooden sign that read POLICE.

Officer Dan Finley was reading a magazine, which, at the small-town station, was practically part of the job description. The young officer was a Puzzle Lady fan. He looked up from his desk, said, "Hi, Chief. Hi, Miss Felton. What's up?"

"Listen, Dan. About Mrs. Fielding—"

"Ida."

"Yeah, Ida."

Dan shook his head. "Terrible thing." He jerked his thumb in the direction of the holding cells. "You gonna let Jason go?"

"Is he awake?"

"He is now."

"Huh?"

"He had a visitor. I suppose she woke him up."

Harper's eyes narrowed. "Becky Baldwin? How'd she know he was here?"

Dan waved the questions away. "No, no, not an attorney. At least I don't think so." He considered. "I suppose she could have been? . . ."

"Dan."

"Sorry. It just never occurred to me. I guess that's prejudice—"

"Dan! Who was it?"

"Oh. A Japanese lady."

Harper swore, immediately apologized to Cora.

Cora smiled. "I've heard worse."

Harper was controlling himself with an effort. "She still here?"

"The Japanese lady? No, she left."

"Where did she go?"

"I don't know."

"Find her."

"Sir?"

"Find her and bring her in."

Dan got up from his desk with a sounds-stupid-but-if-you-say-so attitude. "What if she doesn't want to come?"

"Arrest her."

Jason Fielding smelled like a brewery. To Cora Felton, who had given up drinking, it was an uncomfortable reminder. His eyes were glassy; his hair was unkempt; there was a stain on his shirt-front from some spilled drink or other. He sat on the cot with his head in his hands, rocking back and forth.

He looked up at them through bloodshot eyes. "My wife is dead."

It was somewhere between a question and a statement, the diseased ramblings of an alcohol-riddled brain.

"Who told you that?"

Jason fought to focus. "Lady."

"What lady?"

"Silk. Is she dead?"

"Mr. Fielding, do you know where you are?"

"In jail."

"Do you know why?"

"Had a drink. Threw a chair."

"Threw a chair?"

"Think so. Not sure."

"Hang on a minute, Chief," Cora said. "Jason. The lady who was just here. The silk lady. What did she want to know?"

"If I was Jason. Course I am. Is she dead?"

"What else did the silk lady want to know?"

Jason furrowed his brow, moaned, said, "Bar."

"What bar?" Harper demanded.

"What bar?"

"What bar?"

"Bar."

Harper scowled.

"Mind if I step in here, Chief. You're getting in a rut. She asked you what bar you were drinking in?"

"Yes."

"What did you tell her?"

Before he could answer, Becky Baldwin came swooping in. The young Bakerhaven attorney was holding a briefcase. If it had had a number on its side, she could have passed for a *Deal or No Deal* model.

Becky struck a pose, said, "So?"

"Wait in my office," Harper snapped.

"Wait in your office?"

"Yes," Chief Harper said. "Why aren't you doing that?"

"While you interrogate my client?"

"Jason is your client?"

"He will be after we've had a little talk. If you'd like to give me a few minutes."

Chief Harper exhaled noisily. "No, I do not want to give you a few minutes. You're either his attorney or you're not. If you're not his attorney, I'd like you to wait in my office. I'll be right with you."

"You want to hire me, Jason?"

Jason looked at her. "What for?"

"See?" Becky announced. "He is obviously in need of representation. Have you advised him of his rights?"

"Well—"

"It's a moot point, considering the shape he's in. If a defendant is incapable of understanding his rights, reading them doesn't count. So, which is it? You read 'em and it doesn't count, or you haven't even read 'em?" Becky turned back to the prisoner. "Jason, do you want to hire me?"

"Before he decides, I think you should make it clear that you're an attorney and not a lap dancer," Cora put in helpfully.

"Jason, have they told you your wife is dead?"

"No."

"No?"

"Lady did."

"What lady?"

"Silk lady."

"Great." Becky turned back to the chief. "I'm going to have to ask you to stop interrogating my client until he's able to understand the questions. Is that clear, or do I have to get a court order?"

"Oh, for goodness' sake," Chief Harper said. "This is, in all likelihood, an accidental death. The only thing to keep us from proving that is a bunch of attorneys throwing monkey wrenches into the works."

"Hang on," Cora said. "Becky's a knockout, but I doubt if she counts as a bunch."

"I'd like a word with my client," Becky persisted.

"I haven't heard him hire you yet."

"He was about to when you interrupted."

"Actually, *I* interrupted," Cora said.

"Stop!" Chief Harper said. He pointed to the prisoner, who now had his head between his legs. "You're driving *me* nuts, and I *don't* have a hangover. Think how *he* must feel."

Dan Finley stuck his head in the door. "Got her, Chief."

"Great. Okay, you win, Becky. Have a nice chat. We'll be back. Come on, Cora." Harper held the door for Cora, followed her out. "*This* is going to be fun."

The Sudoku Lady batted her eyes at Chief Harper. "You wished to see me?"

"Yes, I wished to see you. You are a visitor in our town. We want to extend you every courtesy. But you cannot come into our police station, talk to our prisoner, and tell him his wife is dead."

Minami smiled. "Why not?"

"That's not your job. It's my job."

"I do not mind helping."

"You are not helping. I told him his wife was dead and he already knew."

"Then there is no problem. If it is the truth. She is dead, isn't she?"

"Yes."

"Good. I do not mean it is good that she is dead. I mean it is good that we did not tell him she is dead when she is not. That would not be nice, would it?"

Chief Harper opened his mouth, closed it again.

Cora suppressed a smile.

"That is not the point," Harper said. "The point is, you can't come in and start interrogating prisoners. You're not an attorney; you're not with the police; you're not a friend. You're not even a U.S. citizen."

"Only U.S. citizens may talk to prisoners? That is a law I did not know."

"It's not a law."

"That is why I did not know it."

Minami looked perfectly serene in yards and yards of fabric. Her niece looked bored.

"Let me ask you something," Cora said. "You claim that talking to Jason was perfectly innocent and within your rights."

"Yes."

"Good. What did he say?"

"I beg your pardon?"

"What did he tell you? What did you learn? Will you share that information?"

"But of course." Minami settled back in her chair.

"Here we go," Michiko said.

"Did he tell you he was drinking at a bar?" Harper asked.

"Yes, he did."

"The Rainbow Room?"

"Yes. Did he tell you that, too?"

"He did not. By the time I talked to him he was confused and disoriented. I only assumed he told you that because it's where my officer Dan Finley picked you up."

"How did the officer know I was there?"

"He called every bar in town."

"That was smart. You are good at your job."

"I'm just one step behind you." Harper took a breath. "I'm going to have to ask you to cease and desist."

"I beg your pardon?"

"Stop what you're doing."

"Why? The man was in jail when his wife died. Clearly he did not do it."

Becky Baldwin poked her head in the door. "Am I interrupting?"

"Yes," Chief Harper said.

"No," Cora said. "Come on in."

Becky swooped in. "How do you do? I'm Becky Baldwin, attorney at law. You must be the woman who spoke to my client."

"I am Minami, the Sudoku Lady."

Michiko snorted. "Do you have to say that to everyone? You sound like a superhero."

"And this is my niece, Michiko. We had a very nice talk with Mr. Fielding."

"And now you're talking with the police. I'm not sure I like that."

Harper smiled. "Ah. The silver lining. It would appear Minami has not interfered in my business as much as she has in yours."

"Plus," Cora put in, "anything he told her is *not* a confidential communication."

"That's a hell of a thing to spread around," Becky said.

"Why?" Harper said. "Are you advising him not to answer any questions?"

"I don't know what I'm advising him at this point. I'd like to keep my options open."

"Options? What options? The woman fell down and hit her head. Her husband's drunk and in jail. He has the option of staying there and sobering up or going home and sobering up. It doesn't seem a difficult choice to me, and I don't see why he needs a lawyer to make it."

"That's the situation here?"

"Absolutely."

"Are you prepared to rule it was an accidental death?"

"It's not my place to make such a ruling. That's up to the medical examiner and the prosecutor. At the moment there's no reason to assume it was anything else."

"If the autopsy turned up a whacking dose of poison in her stomach, would that change your mind?" Cora said.

Harper gave her a look. "Are you trying to make trouble?"

"I'm just trying to clarify things. And I like to give you and Minami something to talk about."

"We have plenty to talk about, and that's not it. There is no poison involved in the case. I am not *expecting* any poison involved in the case, and there damn well better *not* be any poison involved in the case. If there *is* any poison in the case, I'm going to want to know why you *suspected* poison in the case."

"I don't suspect poison in the case. That was a hypothetical example. If you want my opinion, this is an accidental death, and we can all chalk it up and move on." Cora jerked her thumb at Minami. "Of course, *she* may have other ideas." She gestured to Becky. "And *she* may have other ideas. Clearly, they conflict." She smiled. "Which puts you in the perfect position to do anything you want to. Which is only fitting for a chief of police."

Harper put up his hands. "Wait a minute, wait a minute. Why is *any* of this happening? There is no crime here. Much as you might love to drum one up."

"Me?" Cora said. "I'm not drumming it up. She is. There is one very suspicious circumstance here, Chief, and I hate to spill it in front of these two women, but they've undoubtedly copped to it anyway or they wouldn't be doing this. Jason has a perfect alibi for the time his wife was killed. Perfect. Ironclad. You couldn't draw it up any better. You're his alibi witness. You and the whole damn police force. If I were going to bump off a husband—and God knows, I've wanted to—I can't think of a better plan than to have him apparently killed at a time when I was in jail. Not that I was in jail that often, you understand, still—"

"Cora."

"Anyway, that's undoubtedly what has attracted these two women to this crime. That and the fact that one of them gets to charge a fee."

Harper snorted in exasperation.

Cora smiled. "Hope I set everything straight, Chief. Well, gotta go."

Cora started out. She turned back in the doorway, her eyes twinkling. "You kids have fun."

Becky Baldwin's law office was a second-floor walk-up down the side street over the pizza parlor. Becky had just started up the stairs when a hand reached out and grabbed her. She wheeled around.

It was Cora.

"What are you doing? You scared me to death."

"We need to talk."

"We have nothing to talk about. You sold me out back there."

"That's what I want to talk about."

"Well, you should. I thought we were friends."

"We are friends. We also have a business relationship."

"What's that got to do with it?"

"This is business."

"So it's all right to sell me out if it's business?"

"Let's go in your office. I'd hate for people to hear us squabbling on the stairs."

Becky unlocked the door and let Cora in. Becky's office, small and poorly furnished, gave the impression that business was not good. Indeed, it wasn't. Bakerhaven was a small town. The need for lawyers was not great, even in the best of times. During the financial crisis her client base had shrunk to nothing.

Cora flopped down in the client's chair, took out her cigarettes.

Becky raised her finger. "No. This is your idea. You're here on sufferance. You light that thing, you're going out."

"Relax. We're both on the same side."

"What side is that?"

"The side of truth, justice, and the American way."

Becky glared at her.

"Oh, I forgot. You're a lawyer. We're on the side of your client, *regardless* of truth, justice, and the American way."

"Why are you here?"

"I'm here to help you."

"Help me? You damn near crucified me."

"I'm here to protect you from that dreadful woman."

"What?"

"You saw what she did. She talked to your client. Now she's blabbing to the police."

"You *told* her to blab to the police!"

"I did nothing of the sort. I just said she's under no legal restraint. Which is a shame, because a woman like that *ought* to be under some legal restraint."

"What in the world is she doing here?"

Cora told Becky the story of the Sudoku Lady.

"She's a rival puzzle constructor?"

"*She* thinks she is. We both have sudoku books. Big deal. If hers were doing better than mine, you think I'd go to Japan to meet her?"

"Your book is doing better than hers in Japan?"

"Apparently."

"She has a problem with that?"

"She has lots of problems."

"If her books were doing better than yours over here, would you have a problem with that?"

"I wouldn't even *know* it. You think I give a damn? Here I am, minding my own business, some young upstart comes along—"

"She *is* younger than you, isn't she?"

"She's heard I'm an amateur detective—she wants to take me on solving crime."

"That's ridiculous."

"Yes, it is. She's out to get your client just to prove that she can do it. She's egocentric, ambitious, competitive."

"So?"

"In detective stories, you know how the cops are always trying to convict somebody? They don't seem to care if he's innocent— they just want to clear the crime?"

"You think she's like that?"

"She wants to win. She's over there blabbing to Chief Harper right now, trying to bring your client down."

"You want to stop her?"

"Damn right I want to stop her."

"You want to help me get my client off?"

"Of course, I do."

"Do you care if he's innocent or guilty?"

Cora snorted. "Hell, no. I want to win."

Aaron Grant couldn't believe what he was hearing. Which didn't stop him from enjoying his veal piccata. Still, he was somewhat distracted, much to Sherry's displeasure.

"I'm a newlywed," she protested. "When I cook for you, pay attention. You think civility stops right after the honeymoon?"

"Usually," Cora said. She frowned thoughtfully. "Though, in Melvin's case, it stopped *on* the honeymoon. God, what did I ever see in that man?"

"Murder?" Aaron persisted.

Sherry glared at Cora.

"Very good pork," Cora said.

"It's veal."

"It's very good." She took a bite, chewed. "It's an accidental death. The only thing that points to it not being an accidental death is the fact that she died at a time her husband couldn't have done it. The thing that gets him is he appeared to have an airtight alibi."

"That makes it look like he arranged it," Aaron said.

"He didn't. He's just a poor sot who woke up from the worst blackout drunk of his life."

"You mean if he killed her."

"Either way. If he killed her and doesn't remember or didn't kill her and doesn't remember, it's the same thing. He doesn't know if he killed her."

"If he killed her, it means he had those tendencies. Which would be part of his psyche."

"Oh, please," Cora said. "If I woke up married to a used-car salesman, would you say I had those tendencies?"

Aaron found himself very busy cutting his veal.

Cora's face darkened. "For God's sake. It's bad enough when you kid about my men. When you get embarrassed by them, it's ten times worse. Is it just because you're married? It never bothered you when you were single. See why I have to move out? I'm corrupting the morals of your husband."

"You're moving out?" Aaron said.

"Where have *you* been? Never mind. I know where you've been. This is not a honeymoon cottage. You need your own space. And I need mine."

"I didn't know you felt that way."

"Of course not. You're young; you're in love. You're not cynical yet. I'd like to help you stay that way. You got enough problems with Dennis."

"Cora," Sherry warned.

Aaron frowned. "Dennis? What about Dennis?"

"Didn't she mention it? He's been calling. You wouldn't even know if I hadn't been here spoiling the party."

"What did Dennis want?"

"I don't know," Sherry said. "He called. I hung up."

"Didn't he say anything?"

"I didn't let him say anything. I hung up the phone."

"How'd you know it was him?"

"I recognized his voice."

"Then he must have said something."

Cora smiled, spread her hands. "My work here is done."

"Look at that," Sherry said. "See how neatly she changed the subject. You wouldn't know we were talking about her moving out."

"Actually, we were talking about a murder," Cora said. "I was just digressing from the digression."

"Exactly," Aaron said. "If it's a murder, why didn't I get the story?"

"There's no story. It's not a murder."

"But Chief Harper thinks it is?"

"No, he doesn't."

"But the husband's in jail?"

"On a drunk and disorderly charge."

"Why isn't he out?"

"Because his lawyer won't let him talk."

"He hired Becky Baldwin?"

"Doesn't everyone?"

"He must think he'll be suspected."

"He doesn't think anything. He's drunk and barely conscious. Becky thrust herself on him, and the poor guy never had a chance."

"He didn't call her?"

"Obviously."

"Who tipped her off?"

"Don't look at me. I don't go making trouble."

"You worked for Becky in the past."

"When she hired me. I don't go soliciting employment."

"But you have a relationship. Times are tough. You might throw her a bone."

"Kids," Sherry said. "This is not a debate. Cora's not going to lie about it. Cora, did you tip Becky off? Yes or no?"

"No. If you want my opinion—"

"I do," Aaron said.

"I'd lean on Dan Finley. I know he tips the TV people off."

"That's different. The cops always want to get in good with the media. Lawyers are on the other side."

"Yeah, but Becky's a pretty girl."

Aaron's eyes widened. "Do you mean—?"

"Dan's young, male, single, and he's not blind. Just because he acts like a boy doesn't mean he doesn't think like a man."

"Cora, you can't go," Sherry said. "We'd be lost without these insights."

The phone rang. Sherry got up to answer it.

"If that's Dennis, I want to talk to him," Aaron said.

"It isn't Dennis."

"If it is, give me the phone."

"I can take care of myself."

"I know you can. Just give me the phone."

"You gonna answer that?" Cora said.

"If it's Dennis—"

"If it's Dennis, I'll say, 'Just a minute, here's my husband.' Will that satisfy you?" Sherry picked up the phone and said, "Hello? . . . Now . . . But that's not necessary . . . Very well. A half an hour."

Sherry hung up the phone, cocked her head.

"That wasn't Dennis."

The Sudoku Lady sat on the edge of the couch and sipped her tea. She looked calm and composed and completely at home. "This is very nice."

"Niceness has nothing to do with it," Cora said. "You called and said you were coming. What do you want?"

"What my aunt means to say," Sherry put in quickly, "is to what do we owe the honor of this visit?"

"That's exactly what I meant to say," Cora said. "I couldn't have phrased it better."

"We are here to apologize for this afternoon."

"Apologize for what?" Cora demanded.

"We said we would come to see you, and then we did not. We are not in the habit of making appointments that we do not keep. It is rude. We are sorry. It was an emergency and could not be helped."

"I saw you," Cora said. "Several times. At the house. At the police station. I saw you all day long."

"You did not see me here. As I promised."

"No one is holding you to any promise."

"See," Michiko said, "they don't want us here."

"You are welcome here," Sherry said. "It's just that you have no obligation."

Michiko snorted. "She knows. She does it anyway. She's passive aggressive." She tossed the phrase off with the bored wisdom of a typical teenager. "Where did you get that sweater?"

"At the mall."

"See?" Michiko scrunched her legs up under her on the chair and pouted.

"So," Cora said, "you've apologized for not coming the first time. Your apology is accepted. You're here now, and everything is fine. Promise you won't come a third time to apologize for coming a second time, and all is forgiven."

"You do not wish us here?"

"I do not wish to hear you apologize. All apologies past, present, and future are accepted. Now, can we drop the protocol and talk like human beings?"

"Cora," Sherry warned.

Minami pulled herself up. "I have offended you?"

"Heavens, no," Cora said. "Then you'll want to apologize. Everything is just ducky. That means good, fine, okay. Now then, why are you here? I don't mean here tonight in my house as a result of the accidental occurrences of the day. I mean here in the United States. Why did you come to see me?"

"Ah. You are the Puzzle Lady and I am the Sudoku Lady. It is only natural that we should meet."

"Yeah, yeah," Michiko scoffed. "Big deal. Dueling sudoku divas."

"You're joking," Sherry said. "You've come here for a sudoku contest?"

"See?" Michiko said. "Even her niece thinks that's silly." She cocked her head. "Well, are you going to give it to her or not?"

Cora frowned. "Give me what?"

"Oh, I forget my manners," Minami said. "I have a present for you." She reached into her silk purse and took out a red envelope the size of a greeting card.

Cora frowned. She opened the envelope and pulled out a folded piece of paper. "What's this?"

					8	5	3	
7	8				1			
				6	2			4
		5						
		2			7	9		
3			9				4	
8	2							
							6	
9			4			3	7	

"It's a sudoku," Michiko said impatiently. "From her new book. To show you how clever she is."

Minami started to protest, but the girl cut her off. "She didn't give you the solution. But you don't need it, do you?"

"I think I can handle it," Cora said.

Michiko nodded. "It is hard, but you can do it. There. That's done. Can we get on with it?"

"Forgive me," Cora said, "but get on with what? Why are you here?"

"Ah," Minami said. "In my country I am known. I am the Sudoku Lady. An expert."

Michiko snorted. Her eyes were mocking.

Sherry sympathized. The girl was rude, but she must have been quite sick of her aunt's bragging.

"The price of fame," Cora said. "So what?"

"The police came to me. A man is dead. He was solving a sudoku when he died."

"They wanted you to solve it?"

"That is right."

"And you did?"

"I told them it was stupid. They would not listen. They did not just want it solved. They wanted to know what the numbers meant. They meant nothing. They were just numbers."

"Of course. So you told them that?"

"I did. But they did not like the answer. They wanted the crime to be, how do you say, spectacular."

"Oh, puh-lease," Michiko said. "They did nothing of the kind. They thanked her for her help and sent her on her way. She just wouldn't go."

Cora's eyes widened. "Oh. I see. You solved the crime."

"It was a simple crime. Once you take the sudoku out. If there was no sudoku, the police could solve it. It was a distraction. They thought it was important. I knew it was not."

"You solved the crime without the sudoku and the police weren't happy about it. Have you assisted them with other crimes?"

"They have not asked."

"Hah!" Michiko snorted. "Just like I did not ask to come on this trip. But here I am. My aunt is always bothering the police."

"I do not bother the police."

"No. You help them against their will. It is entirely different." Minami turned to Cora. "I am sure that is not what you do."

"What are you talking about?"

"You help the police. Whether there is a puzzle or not."

"Who told you that?"

"It is on TV. In Japan. Special documentary of the week. Do you not remember?"

Cora did. Japanese filmmakers had followed her around and questioned her about her puzzle-making expertise, always a ticklish subject since she had none. "Yes. I remember the questions. It was all about puzzles."

"It was all about crime. First we see you talking about puzzles. Then we see you on American TV talking about crime."

"American TV?"

"On the news. You are in front of the police station. You are in court. You are at the scene of a crime."

"You mean they used footage from Rick Reed and the Channel 8 news crew?"

"A handsome young man. Not very bright."

"That's Rick Reed."

"I see you on TV. I want to invite you to our country. Show

you how our police work. Ask you to solve a crime. But that would not be fair. You are American. You do not know our country. You probably do not speak Japanese."

"Good guess."

"So. I know English. I will come here."

"You came here to solve a crime?"

"Is it not fun? It is like your American reality shows. *Survivor. The Amazing Race.*"

"You're challenging me to solve a crime?"

"See?" Michiko said. "The Battle of the Century: The Sudoku Lady versus the Puzzle Lady."

"I'm not crazy about the billing."

"I beg your pardon?"

"This is ridiculous. There is no crime to solve."

"Oh, but there is. Ida Fielding. I think it is a murder. You think it is not. One of us is right. The winner must prove she is right."

"That's not going to happen."

"Why not?"

"You can't prove he did it because he didn't. I can't prove he didn't because that's proving a negative."

"You do not prove he did not kill her. You prove someone else did."

"No one did. It was an accidental death."

"Then you prove that. Do we have a bet?"

"Good lord. You're serious."

"Why would I not be serious? Do we have a bet?"

"If I say yes, will you leave?"

"Cora."

Minami stood. "We are leaving." She bowed. "Now we go, and tomorrow we solve a crime. Yes?"

"Great," Cora said dryly.

"We are agreed? Yes? You are content with the arrangement? You have no questions?"

Michiko yawned and stretched. "I got a question. What time does the mall close?"

Minami took one look at the cotton top her niece tried on in the mall Gap and declared, "You are not wearing that!"

Michiko looked betrayed. "*She* was wearing it."

"She is a grown-up. You are a little girl."

"I am *not* a little girl." Michiko stamped her foot. "Little girls play with dolls and are afraid of frogs. I am a *big* girl. I need big girl clothes."

"You are not that big."

"I am not that little."

Minami was unmoved. "It is too tight. It makes you look like a lady of the street."

"Lady of the street?"

"You are a big girl. You know what I mean."

"Make up your mind. Am I a big girl or a little girl?"

"You are a big girl in a little shirt. It does not fit you."

"It is stretch material."

"It is stretched very thin. It is not decent."

"Fine!" Michiko glared at her aunt, grabbed a wine red pull-over, and stamped off toward the dressing room.

Minami walked over and examined the pile of shirts from which it had come. She picked one up, exhaled sharply. It was skintight *and* scoop-necked.

Michiko left the store semi-victorious in low-rise jeans and a purple tank top. She was quite pleased with herself until another girl wearing exactly the same thing caused her to reevaluate the situation. The girl was too young, not particularly attractive, and had no sense of style. Which was certainly not the fault of the clothes, though how the girl had fallen into them was beyond Michiko. *She* looked good.

Minami stopped in front of a Rite Aid drugstore. "I must go in here."

Michiko waved her hand. "Go."

"You will come, too."

"I will be in there." Michiko pointed to the Virgin Megastore.

Minami was not quite sure what a Virgin Megastore was. She didn't like the sound of it but didn't want to show her ignorance. "But nowhere else."

"I just want to look at CDs."

"And you will be in the store and nowhere else."

"Yes, yes, nowhere else," Michiko cried impatiently.

Minami, who'd felt a headache coming on ever since they got to the mall, went off in search of Advil.

Michiko, happy and free in her new American clothes, trotted into the Megastore. She headed for the wall where the top-fifty albums were displayed, pulled on a headset, and began listening to that new Pink CD she knew her aunt wouldn't like.

Michiko was on the second track when she looked up to find someone smiling at her.

The young man had long hair like a rock star. His white shirt was open at the neck, and he had removed his tie. His cocked head, which made his hair hang down at an angle, gave him a raffish, appealing look. Michiko wondered if he practiced it in the mirror. She smiled nonetheless.

"Hi," he said.

Her aunt had told her not to talk to strangers, a clear invitation to do so. "Hi."

"Pardon me, but I know I've seen your mother somewhere before."

Michiko made a face. "She is not my mother."

"Oh?"

"She is worse than my mother. She is my aunt."

"Why is she worse than your mother?"

"She tells me what to do. And gets mad if I do not do it."

"How is that worse than your mother?"

"My mother does not tell me what to do."

"Why not?"

"She is not here."

He smiled.

She stuck her nose in the air. "You are laughing at me?"

"I'm not laughing *at* you. You made a joke."

Michiko pouted. "I am glad it is funny for you. It is not funny for me. It is like being in jail."

His eyes twinkled. "Have you ever been in jail?"

"No."

"Then how would you know?"

He was teasing her. Michiko didn't like being teased. "My aunt said I shouldn't talk to strangers."

"I'm not a stranger. I know your aunt. I just don't know from where."

"She is famous."

"Oh?"

"She is the Sudoku Lady." Michiko made a face. "Big deal. I cannot go anywhere that people do not think they know her. You do not know her. You just think you do. Because she wears a silk kimono. Like a costume."

"At least she doesn't have a big red *S* on her chest." Michiko looked puzzled. "You know. Like Superman. We have our own superhero in town. The Puzzle Lady. Did you know that?"

"Of course. My aunt came to see her."

"She did?"

"Yes. All the way from Japan. And I have to come along."

"You didn't want to come to America?"

"Not to be a babysitter."

"Your aunt has children?"

"No. To babysit her. I am looking out for her. She thinks she is looking out for me. It is so stupid."

"Why does she need looking out for?"

"She thinks she can do anything. A woman fell and hit her head. Everyone says it was an accident. She says it was murder."

"Really?"

"If I do not watch her, she will get in trouble. And—"

"Michiko!"

Minami was glaring at her from the doorway.

"Oh. Gotta go." She hurried to rejoin her aunt.

"Who is that man?"

"No one."

"You're not supposed to talk to strangers."

"He is not a stranger. He knew you."

"I do not know him. I cannot leave you alone for a minute."

The two of them went out the door, the teenager whining about overprotective aunts.

Dennis Pride watched them go. Well, that was interesting. He wondered what two Japanese women were doing calling on Sherry and Cora. So she was the Sudoku Lady. Whatever that was.

Dennis had been in a funk ever since Sherry got married. Yes, she'd divorced him and, yes, he'd gotten married again, to her best friend Brenda Wallenstein. But that was different. Entirely different. He still cared for Sherry. Still wanted her. He'd gotten married because she didn't want him. But he was there for her. Always. Ready to pick up the pieces. His marriage meant nothing because it was no bar to his desire.

Hers was different. Entirely different. She hadn't gotten married *in spite of* wanting him. She'd gotten married because she *didn't* want him.

At least that's what she thought. Dennis knew it wasn't true— that sooner or later she'd come to her senses. Indeed, her marriage had given him hope. It was just the spur she needed to see that she was on the wrong path. Married life, Dennis thought, could soon sour her on that young reporter, a man not worthy of her in any way. She would see what a mistake she'd made, and she would want to fix it. When she did, he'd be there waiting.

And now this. A rival for Cora Felton. A Japanese counterpart. With a precocious teenage niece. That was good. That had to be good. Anything that stirred the waters, that created controversy. If there was a rivalry between the two, how sweet would it be if he could beat them both?

At long last, things were finally breaking his way.

Chapter

Jason Fielding was somewhat overwhelmed. His wife was dead. He was a murder suspect. Now he wasn't, but his wife was still dead. The police had let him back into his house, and now he was in his living room with a Japanese woman who looked like a Japanese woman, in a colorful silk kimono, and a Japanese girl who looked like an American girl, in typical teenage attire. These two women, real or imaginary, were in his living room, the same living room where his wife had died, if she was indeed dead, if it wasn't an alcohol-induced fantasy dredged up from the deep subconscious of his being as a warning never under any circumstances to drink again.

The Japanese woman was talking, enumerating the very points of confusion in his mind. "I am sorry that your wife is dead. It is a tragedy. But I am glad that the police let you go."

Jason blinked. "I saw you in jail," he said. He wondered if it was true.

"And now you are out of jail. And now we can talk."

That triggered another memory. "My lawyer told me not to talk to anyone."

Minami smiled. "Your lawyer is Miss Rebecca Baldwin?"

"Yes,"

"She told you not to talk to the police. Because they might not understand, and then they would keep you in jail. She did not say you could not talk to me." Minami nodded in agreement with herself, then steamed ahead as if there had been no digression. "The police believe you killed your wife. Now we must find out who did."

Jason frowned. "Who did?"

"Yes."

"No one did. It was an accident."

"That would be nice. Not that she had an accident. But it would be nice if no one wished her dead."

"Don't be silly. Who would want to hurt her?"

"That is what we must determine. What do you have that one might wish to steal?"

"Nothing."

"No cash? No jewels? No coin or stamp collection?"

"No."

"May I see your study?"

"Why?"

Michiko had twisted herself into a pretzel, was tugging on her foot. "Oh, let her. It's the quickest way to get rid of her. Just show her what she wants."

Jason got up, led Minami and Michiko down the hall into his den. It was poorly furnished, with an ancient computer, a tiny TV, a battered bookcase that held more assorted junk than books, a desk chair and an easy chair. There was no table or sideboard.

Minami glanced around. "So. Where do you hide it?"

"What?"

"Your alcohol. You do not have a bar. You like to drink. Your wife did not like you to drink. You hide it. Where?"

Jason started to flare up, then sighed, shrugged, pointed to the bottom drawer.

Minami jerked it open, pulled out a half pint of whiskey and a shot glass. "Ah. Like the American private eye."

"So? No one broke in to steal my booze."

"Of course not. What else do you hide?"

"Nothing."

"Nothing? You do not have a safe in the wall?"

"Don't be silly."

"Why is that silly? What else is hidden in this room?"

"I told you. Nothing."

"I see." Minami bent over, wrenched open the bottom drawer on the other side.

It was full of men's magazines.

"So. Your wife knew about these?"

Michiko pressed forward. "Let me see."

"There is nothing to see," Minami said, slamming the drawer. "Is there, Mr. Fielding? Now, about what else did you lie?"

"Nothing." Jason's face was flushed with embarrassment. "That's enough. Please leave."

Minami nodded. "Yes. I am done with this room."

She went out the door, headed toward the back of the house.

"Hey! Where are you going?"

"This is the kitchen?"

"Stay out of there."

"There is something you do not want me to see in the kitchen?"

"I don't want you in my house. If you don't leave, I'll call the police."

Minami patted him on the cheek. "That would not be wise. There is a back door?"

"Yes. Why?"

"Because the front door is not damaged. There are two possibilities. Your wife let the killer in. Or the killer broke in through the back. We must see which is true."

Minami swept through the pantry to the back door. It had a top lock with a sliding bolt. "You keep this locked?"

"Yes, I keep it locked. It is locked now; it was locked then."

Minami unlocked the back door, inspected the lock on the knob. "There are no signs of forced entry. If the killer got in this way, it was because the door was open."

"Well, it wasn't."

"*You* did not leave it open. You cannot speak for your wife."

Along one wall of the pantry was a freezer chest. Minami lifted the lid and peered in. "You do not have much food."

"So what?"

"Such a big freezer. And you have only boxes of frozen peas." Minami leaned over, inspected the bottom. "What is that?"

"What?"

In the frost built up in the bottom of the freezer was a reddish stain. "That looks like blood."

Jason shrugged. "Some meat leaked."

"You have no meat."

"I have no meat now. I had it. It leaked. I ate it. Big deal."

"Then why is there none? If you keep meat in the freezer to eat, why do you not have any?"

"It's out of season."

"What?"

"Deer-hunting season." Jason sounded exasperated. "In deer-hunting season, I fill the freezer with meat. When the meat is gone, I don't use the freezer until next season. Are you satisfied? Is that enough for you?"

"You hunt the deer?"

"Yes."

"In hunting season?"

"Yes."

"You have a gun?"

"I have a rifle."

"Let me see."

"No."

"Do the police know you have a gun?"

Jason said nothing.

"If you do not show me the gun, then I must tell the police that you have a gun that you do not wish to show. They will want to see it and—"

"All right, all right."

Jason led them to a hall closet under the stairs. He reached behind a set of golf clubs and pulled out a rifle. "There. You satisfied?"

"Let me see." Minami grabbed the rifle, raised the barrel to her nose, sniffed. "This rifle has been fired."

"Of course it's been fired. I use it to hunt."

"It has been fired recently."

"No. I . . ."

"What?"

"I do some target practice. Down at the dump."

"They let you shoot at the dump?"

"No. Sunday. When the dump is closed. What difference does it make? My wife wasn't shot."

"You are sure of that?"

Jason wasn't sure of anything. His head was coming off. Everything the crazy Japanese lady said seemed to make things worse and worse. Maybe he shouldn't be talking to her. Maybe it wasn't just the police. She was the one who said it was all right. What would his lawyer say? Did he have a lawyer? Was that part real? He fished in his pocket, came out with Becky Baldwin's business card.

Jason marched into the living room, picked up the phone.

"What are you doing?" Minami said.

"Calling my lawyer."

Michiko's eyes twinkled. "Hah!"

"Well, we must be going," Minami said, and herded her smiling niece out the door.

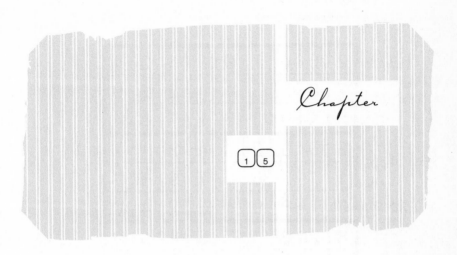

Chapter

1 5

Cora was looking through the real estate section in the morning paper. It wasn't a huge task. In a town the size of Bakerhaven, the real estate section was half a page. Nothing seemed appropriate. Everything was either a room in someone's house or a building the size of a college dorm. Or a summer rental while the family went to Europe. No small cottage with modest heat and electric bills suitable for single occupancy.

The only alternative was to get her New York apartment back. The couple who sublet would be shocked after so many years to suddenly find themselves evicted, especially with the rents Manhattan apartments were commanding these days. Cora hated to do it. She had a heart of gold. On the other hand, maybe she should raise the rent.

Cora folded the paper and threw it on the coffee table. The red envelope was lying there. Cora pulled out the sudoku from Min-ami. The girl said it was hard. It looked challenging, but Cora was good at sudoku. She picked up a pencil, went to work.

It took her nearly fifteen minutes.

2	6	4	7	9	8	5	3	1
7	8	3	5	4	1	6	2	9
5	1	9	3	6	2	7	8	4
6	9	5	2	3	4	8	1	7
1	4	2	6	8	7	9	5	3
3	7	8	9	1	5	2	4	6
8	2	6	1	7	3	4	9	5
4	3	7	8	5	9	1	6	2
9	5	1	4	2	6	3	7	8

Cora scanned the answer to make sure she was right. That was the only problem with the damn things. If you were sloppy and didn't watch out, you might wind up with two sevens in the same line.

The phone rang.

Cora picked it up in the kitchen.

It was Chief Harper. "Better get in here."

Cora padded down the hall to the office where Sherry was working on a crossword. "I gotta go to town."

"Damn. I'm almost finished with this puzzle."

"So, stay here."

"I need the car. I'll have to drop you off and come back."

They headed for town, Sherry driving.

"When I move out, you'll have to get your own car."

"I can use Aaron's."

"Then you'd have to drive him to work."

"Oh. I guess you better stay."

"For a car? That's a dumb reason."

"What's Harper want?"

"I don't know. He didn't sound happy."

"It's the economy," Sherry said. "No one's happy these days."

"Tell me about it."

Sherry pulled up in front of the police station. "How long you gonna be?"

"I have no idea. Why don't you come on in?"

"What if Chief Harper doesn't like it?"

"Then you'll leave."

Dan Finley was at his desk.

"Chief wants to see me," Cora said.

"Yeah, I heard."

"You know what he wants?"

"I think he needs rescuing."

Cora raised her eyebrows. "Oh?"

"See for yourself."

Cora and Sherry slipped into the office. Chief Harper sat behind his desk. He looked harried.

Minami, in full regalia, sat opposite. Her niece, slumped in a chair next to her, looked bored.

On the other side of Minami sat a man in a custom-tailored three-piece suit, a pink shirt, and a purple tie. Cora's eyes practically crossed. She had to refocus them to look at his face. It was pudgy and thin at the same time, a remarkable achievement. Puffy eyes, bulbous lips, but sunken cheeks. He looked like something out of a forties' monster movie. Only they were in black and white.

Cora jerked her thumb. "Who's he?"

The man was on his feet, smiling grotesquely and extending a hand. "Irving Swartzman," he said. It was a pronouncement. "I represent the Sudoku Lady."

Cora frowned at Minami. "You brought a lawyer?"

"He is not my lawyer."

"Of course not. I am her agent. I am here to represent her rights."

"Rights? What rights?"

Michiko rolled her eyes. "This is really stupid."

"So," Cora said, "you brought your niece and your agent. That's hardly fair. My niece *is* my agent. It's three against two."

Chief Harper put up his hands. "Please. I have a small problem here. We have the matter of Ida Fielding's death. I would like to clear it up as quickly and quietly as possible. This man, on the other hand, would like to exploit it."

Swartzman's eyes widened. The effect was eerie. "Did I say that? I merely said that credit should be given where credit's due. If the Sudoku Lady has solved a crime that otherwise would have gone unnoticed, that's a story. You can't expect me to ignore it."

"Wait a minute," Cora said. "What do you mean, 'solved a crime'?"

Chief Harper cleared his throat. "Miss, ah, Minami has made some rather disturbing allegations."

"Oh?"

"I want to check them out before I take any action. Particularly since the medical examiner has ruled Mrs. Fielding's death accidental."

"It wasn't?" Cora said.

"Minami disputes that finding. She has some evidence which leads her to believe—"

"Evidence? Where did she get evidence?"

Harper sighed. "Why don't we let her tell it?"

Minami smiled. "Mrs. Fielding was murdered. Everything points to it. The husband appears to have an alibi. But does he? His alibi is too good to be true. It is perfect. It is, how do you say, dressed in iron."

"Ironclad. Yes, he does," Cora said. "It is not because he is guilty. It is because he is innocent."

"So, I ask around. Is the husband having an affair? That would be a strong motive. Alas, he is not. Is the wife having an affair? Here we have ground that is more fertile. Mrs. Fielding had no job. What is she doing while the husband is at work?"

"Someone comes to the house?" Cora said.

"No. That would not be discreet. The neighbors would see. No one comes to the house. Mrs. Fielding goes out."

"That's all you've got?" Cora scoffed. "I go out in the afternoon. Does that mean I'm having an affair? I wish. I go shopping. Run errands. Just like everyone else."

Minami conceded the point. "Of course, there could be a logical explanation. Or there could not."

"Come on," Harper said, "tell her what you told me."

"Ah. Mr. Fielding has, in his pantry, a freezer cabinet. Long and deep. With a lid that lifts. It is nearly empty. In the bottom there is blood."

"So?"

"Minami thinks the body was put in the deep freeze to alter the time of death," Harper said. "On the basis of the blood and the fact that there's room for a body because the freezer was nearly empty."

"That's very interesting," Cora said. "Stupid but interesting."

"Ah!" Minami smiled. "You mean to insult me. But I forgive you. You are unhappy you did not think of it first."

"The only one unhappy is the chief. Have you investigated this claim?"

"That's a problem," Harper said.

"No kidding. This is an accidental death. The only evidence you have is blood in the freezer. You can't even prove it's human blood. To do that, you'd have to test it. You have to get a warrant. You can't get a warrant unless it's a crime. If it's a crime, you gotta advise Mr. Fielding of his rights, and then Becky Baldwin's involved, and it's gonna take an act of God to get that warrant."

"If the blood is from a deer, the husband has nothing to hide."

"Tell it to his lawyer. She doesn't know the blood's from a deer. She only knows what he tells her. What if he's lying?"

"It is not smart to lie to your lawyer."

"Criminals are not always smart," Cora said dryly. "The point is, no lawyer in her right mind is ever going to let you test that blood. So you are in an extremely unpromising no-win situation." She frowned. "Which I suppose is the only kind. Or is there such thing as a *promising* no-win situation?"

Harper grimaced, rubbed his forehead. "Please. I'm the one in a no-win situation. I went to work this morning—everything was fine. Suddenly my nicely tied up accidental death, the one I just shoved the paperwork for into a file marked CLOSED, is back on the table, and worse than ever. How in the world do I get out of this?"

Irving Swartzman smiled snidely. "My client is extremely sorry to make trouble. In her country, the police do not object to doing their job."

Harper opened his mouth, closed it again, and snorted, not unlike, Cora noted, a fire-breathing dragon.

"Hang on, Chief. I got this one." Cora cocked her head at Minami. "Say we do the test and it's human blood. You say that proves Mrs. Fielding was in the freezer chest. But is that more likely than that it's blood from where Jason cut himself carving up a deer?"

Minami smiled. "A DNA test—"

"Now you want a DNA test?" Harper was fit to be tied.

Cora put up her hand. "No one's testing anything. We're talking hypothetically here. Say it's human blood. Hypothetically. It's hypothetical human blood. Say it's the wife's blood. Say it proves the wife didn't just happen to *bleed* in the freezer; she was actually *in* the freezer. You claim that was done to alter the time of death?"

"Of course."

"Which would be invaluable because the husband was in jail, giving him a perfect alibi. That's all well and good." Cora shrugged. "One small problem. Putting the body in the freezer chest *lowers* the body temperature. It makes the time of death appear *earlier* than it actually was. If Jason killed his wife, put the body in the freezer for an hour, then set the stage and got arrested, it wouldn't make it appear the crime happened while he was in jail. It would make it appear the crime happened well *before* he was in jail. It would, in fact, make his alibi worthless. To make it appear she was killed while he was in jail, he'd have to find a way to *raise* her body temperature."

Harper frowned. "That's right." He smiled. "Hey, that's right. Altering the time of death couldn't possibly help him."

"The only way it would work," Cora said, "was if he got out

of jail, went home, killed his wife, stuck her in the freezer for an hour, pulled her out, and pretended to discover the body. The lower body temperature would make it seem like she was killed while he was still in jail. But that didn't happen here. The guy was still in jail when the body was found. Isn't that right?"

"Yes, it is." Harper raised his voice. "Dan!"

The young officer stuck his head in the door. "Chief?"

"Jason never went home, did he? He was in jail from the time he was arrested in the bar until we told him his wife was dead?"

"Yeah, why?"

"Just double-checking. Thanks, Dan."

Finley went out, closed the door.

"So," Harper said, "that should put an end to that."

Michiko yawned sullenly. "Can we go now?"

Minami's nose was in the air. "Not at all. Miss Felton has shown how it could not work in one particular way. That does not mean it could not work in another way."

Harper groaned. "Oh, come on."

"What other way?" Cora said.

"Mrs. Fielding has a lover. He is married. He wishes to break off the affair. Mrs. Fielding will not let him. She threatens to tell his wife if he does not stay with her. He cannot have that. What is he to do? He is like the man in the movie. The American movie. Where the man has an affair with the woman and she will not let him go because she is not right in the head."

"Michael Douglas and Glenn Close. *Fatal Attraction*," Michiko prompted impatiently.

"Yes, it is like *Fatal Attraction*. Mrs. Fielding will not let go of this man. But it is not a movie. He is not the hero, the star, the good man in the movie. He is a bad man. If the woman will not let him free, he will free himself of her. What does he do? He sees the husband drinking in a bar. The husband is drunk, gets into a fight. Perhaps he even helps to start the fight. The husband is arrested. The lover makes sure the husband is in prison, then goes to see the wife. He kills her, puts her body in the freezer for an hour. Sets the scene and leaves the house. The time of death is changed. It will look like the husband killed his wife, went to the bar and got arrested so he will have an alibi for the time she is killed. He was too stupid to know the medical examiner could tell the time of death."

Cora shook her head. "That's convoluted, even for me."

"It is fantastic, yes? And yet it works. If the police think it is an accidental death, that is fine. If the police believe it is a murder, the person with the opportunity is the husband, not the lover. It is the perfect crime."

Chief Harper said, "Cora?"

"Yes?"

"What about it?"

"What about it? That is the most ridiculous, farfetched, double-think I ever heard. The idea a person would do such a thing. It defies credulity. It is the type of plot that when I read it in a book—"

"I know, I know, you throw the damn thing across the room. But would it work?"

Cora nearly gagged. "Yes, it *could* work. And walking around Times Square in a signboard WILL MARRY RICH MAN FOR CASH could work, too, but that doesn't mean I'm going to try it. The likelihood of such an occurrence is so remote—"

"But it *could* work?"

Cora's mouth snapped shut. She gawked at the chief in helpless frustration.

Irving Swartzman hopped to his feet. "Excellent! Our work here is done. Come, ladies. Let's leave the police chief to his job." The agent smirked. "Now that he knows what it is."

Minami marched proudly out of the office, her niece trailing insolently along behind her.

"Technically you won," Sherry pointed out.

Cora sat sulking in the passenger seat. "In what way did I win?"

"Well, she said Jason killed his wife. You said he didn't. It would appear she was wrong and you were right."

"I said it was an *accident*. I didn't say she was killed by someone else."

"Neither of you did. It was a straightforward bet. She bet she could prove he did it. You bet you could prove he didn't. *She* proved he didn't. Therefore she failed to prove he did. Therefore you win."

"Is that like a Pyrrhic victory?"

"What do you know about Pyrrhic victories?"

"They're not as good as real ones."

Parnell Hall

"Cora . . ."

"That arrogant, insufferable, kimono-wearing woman. I can't say that. It sounds racist. That arrogant, insufferable, sudoku-making woman."

"That could describe you. Good thing you're not arrogant and insufferable."

"Oh, nasty girl. When you were single, you didn't have such a lip."

"I'm trying to jolt you out of your self-induced doldrums into the real world."

"Self-induced doldrums."

"Okay. Competitive-amateur-detective-theory-induced doldrums. The point is, this is a big deal about nothing."

"Chief Harper doesn't think it's about nothing."

"Why?"

"Are you kidding me? That woman just threw a bloodstain in his lap. He's gotta ignore it or deal with it. Dealing with it is an immensely complicated waste of time. Ignoring it is like walking in legal quicksand. If he ignores it and something comes of it, that's the type of omission that could cost a cop his job."

"What do you think he's gonna do?"

"I have no idea."

"He's clearly going to ignore it."

"Why do you say that?"

"Because he let you walk out of there."

"You were with me. He's not going to incriminate himself in front of a witness."

"Incriminate himself?"

"You wanna bet he calls me back in?"

"I don't think you wanna be betting. Betting is how you got into this whole mess."

Cora described Sherry in terms that would have impressed your average drill sergeant.

Sherry said nothing, piloted the Toyota around the curve.

After a while, Cora said, "I can't let her get away with it."

"Oh, no."

"I can't, Sherry. I have Chief Harper to think of. If I did nothing and he got fired, I'd feel awful."

"Plus Minami would win."

"That's not the point. True, rubbing her nose in it would be an added bonus. It's really for Chief Harper."

"What do you have to do?"

"What I have to do is prove Mrs. Fielding wasn't having an affair."

"Isn't that next to impossible?"

"Why?"

"It's proving a negative. Isn't that what you always say? If she's having an affair, it's easy to prove. If she's not having an affair, you have to prove there was no opportunity whatsoever for her to have an affair. Which is damn near impossible."

"You're learning," Cora said.

"I'm glad to hear it. The point is, how do you plan to do it?"

"I'll start with the neighbors."

"Don't you think Minami's done that?"

"Yeah. Maybe I should just ask *her*," Cora said sarcastically. "According to Minami, the woman never had visitors but often went out."

"Does that mean the neighbors are no help?"

"*You're* certainly no help."

Sherry smiled. "Nothing like competition to bring out the best in you."

"Yeah, right."

Sherry turned into the drive.

There was a black rental car parked in front of the house.

"Who the hell is that?" Cora said.

"I have no idea."

"Expecting someone?"

"No."

"If that's our Japanese friend, I'm going to send her packing."

Sherry pulled up next to the car and stopped.

Dennis Pride got out.

Cora flung open the door, hopped out, and put herself between Dennis and her niece.

"Sherry, call the cops!"

Dennis put up his hand. "Please."

"That's closer than a hundred yards."

"I need to talk to you."

"No, you need to leave. Sherry, get inside!"

"Dennis, please."

"Don't talk to him!" Cora snapped. "You're just playing into his hands. Go on. Get inside."

"I'm not leaving you alone with him."

Cora reached into her drawstring purse and pulled out her gun. "I'll be fine. If he doesn't leave, I'll shoot him."

Dennis smiled. "No, you won't."

"Wanna bet?"

"It's not even loaded."

Cora pointed the gun at the sky, pulled the trigger. The report was deafening. She trained the smoking gun on Dennis. "Change your mind?"

"Now, see here."

"Sherry, make the call."

"I'm trying to tell you something. Don't you want to know that Japanese woman's been snooping around?"

"Good-bye, Dennis."

"I did a little snooping myself. Guess what I found out?"

Cora glowered at him. Still, she couldn't help asking, "What's that?"

"Mrs. Fielding had a boyfriend."

Chapter

1 7

Steve Preston was a handsome young man, with a square jaw and a crewcut, and lithe muscles rippling under his fashionably casual suit. "Uh oh. What's wrong?"

"Why should anything be wrong?"

"You're the Puzzle Lady. When you show up, people die."

"I wondered how long it would take to get that reputation. As it happens, someone *is* dead. Mrs. Fielding."

"Oh."

"You know her?"

"Sure. Jason's wife."

Cora raised an ironic eyebrow. "Yeah. That's probably the best way to refer to her."

"What do you mean by that?"

"Rumor has it you knew her better than you knew Jason." Cora shrugged. "Unless you have some proclivities I'm not aware of."

"Now, see here—"

Cora grimaced, shook her finger. "Bad move. When a person begins lecturing an interrogator, it's a sure sign a question hit home. Let's save some time. You and Ida Fielding were having an affair. She's dead. You're married, so you can't let on you care. It's only me. I'm on your side. I could give you a course on home-wrecking one-oh-one. So, cut the crap and let's talk turkey. Otherwise, you can do your talking to the police."

"No police."

"Fine. Did you see Mrs. Fielding the night she died?"

"No."

"Try again."

"Yes."

"Better answer. If you saw her at her house, the neighbor would know. The neighbor didn't. Where did you see her?"

"At the mall."

"At the mall?"

"Yes."

"When was that?"

"Seven thirty. Quarter to eight."

"No, no, no. I don't mean at suppertime. I mean later, after Jason went out."

"I didn't see her then."

"Someone did."

"No one did. It was an accident."

"What if it wasn't? What if she was killed?"

"Then Jason did it."

"Jason has an alibi. He's also got a lawyer. You don't. A lawyer's a huge advantage in a situation like this. Particularly getting in on the ground floor. By the time the cops get to you, Jason will have established a whole bunch of stuff you'll have a hard time disproving."

"What are you talking about?"

"How do you fool the neighbor?"

"Huh?"

"You must have some way of getting into the house without Mrs. Snoopedygidget getting wise. What do you do—cut through the neighbor's yard, sneak up to the back door? Where do you park your car then?"

Steve's eyes flicked.

"God, I'd love to play poker with you," Cora said. "You don't have a game, do you?"

"What?"

"So, your wife doesn't know about the affair. Where does she think you go?"

"Leave my wife out of this."

"There's a nice phrase. You say it to Mrs. Fielding much? Bet it came up a lot."

"I'm going to ask you to leave."

"Of course you are." Cora smiled. "Seen any Japanese women lately?"

"Huh?"

"Don't worry. You will. If that moron Dennis could find you, they can't be far behind."

"What are you talking about?"

"I'm just saying you better start working on your alibi. And guess what, it's not just from eleven o'clock on anymore."

"What?"

Cora smiled. "Ask the Japanese woman."

Michiko snuck out of the Country Kitchen dining room to meet Dennis Pride, who had dropped in for a drink after work. Though "dropped in" was perhaps the wrong choice of words, gave the impression Dennis was just passing by. In point of fact, his last client was in Westport, a good forty-five-minute drive and not in the right direction. No matter. The man knew where he wanted to drink.

Dennis was glad to see her. He already had the genial expansiveness of a man on his second scotch. "Oh, look who's here. Your auntie let you out?"

"She's in the dining room."

"Eating?"

"We just ordered."

"What are you having?"

"The prime rib."

"Good choice. Unless you're a vegetarian. You're not a vegetarian, are you?"

"Don't be stupid."

"Can't help it. I was born that way."

Michiko giggled. "You're silly."

"Your aunt solved the crime yet?"

"What crime?"

"That's right. The police still think it's an accident. You want a drink?"

"No."

"You're not old enough, are you?"

"I just don't want a drink."

"So what's your story?"

"What do you mean?"

"Come on. Young girl like you. Hanging out with your aunt. Doesn't seem like much of a vacation."

"It's not a vacation."

"What is it?"

"It's a trip to America."

"Yeah, but it's not much fun. No kids your age."

Michiko stuck out her chin. "I'm not a kid."

"Of course not. But you're not an old lady, either. What are you doing here?"

"Having dinner."

"Now *you're* being silly. What are you doing in Bakerhaven? Not exactly a prime vacation spot. Unless you're a rabid antique collector. Are you a rabid antique collector?"

"You are teasing me."

"Yes, and you love it. Gotta be a break from looking out for your aunt. What's her trouble? She drinks? Does drugs? Picks up teenage boys?"

"That is not nice."

"The boys like it."

"You are being silly again."

"You're being evasive. Why do you travel with your aunt? Is she your legal guardian?"

Michiko frowned. "What do you mean?"

"Do you have parents?"

"Everyone has parents."

"Are your parents alive?"

"Yes, of course."

"No 'of course' about it. People die. Sometimes they get killed. Like Mrs. Fielding."

"Do you think she was killed?"

"What do you think?"

"You ask a lot of questions."

"I always do when women try to pick me up in bars."

Michiko's mouth fell open. "I am not trying to pick you up."

"Of course not. You just happened to come in here. You're not having a drink. You've already ordered dinner. Your prime rib's probably sitting there getting cold. You're not trying to pick me up at all."

"You are rude."

"Of course I am. If I was nice, you wouldn't like me."

"Why do you say such silly things?"

"You have parents in Japan and you came here with your aunt, but it wasn't for fun because you're not having any. I keep thinking you're along to keep her out of trouble."

"You are wrong."

"Is her English bad? Do you have to interpret for her?"

"Michiko!"

Their heads turned.

Minami stood in the archway to the dining room. Arms out, face stern, yards of silk making her look like a predatory bird. "What are you doing? Our food is at the table. You are not. Instead, you are here. Is this not the young man from the mall? How dare you, sir! My niece is but a child."

"Mi-na-mi!" Michiko whined.

"No more!" Minami pointed imperiously. "Go!"

Michiko glared at her aunt and, tossing her head, sulked and pouted her way from the room.

"Leave my niece alone. She is under age."

"How old is she?"

"That is not your concern."

"She was telling me why you need her here. I thought it might be to interpret, but you speak very well. Is it to keep you out of jail?"

It seemed to Dennis that Minami's eyes flicked. She glared at him then turned to go.

"Did you know Mrs. Fielding had a boyfriend?"

Minami stopped.

Dennis grinned. "You must not have, since he hadn't seen you yet."

She turned back. "What are you talking about?"

"The Puzzle Lady's already seen him. Can the Sudoku Lady be far behind? Only thing is, she thought I followed you there. Like I have no skills of my own. So, you're behind her. And she's behind me. And the cops haven't got a clue. They're behind all of us."

"Who is this man?"

"Ah, now you're interested? I thought you wanted me to leave you alone."

"You are impertinent."

Dennis grinned. "Yes, I am. Feels great, by the way. But that's what winning is all about."

"I don't believe you. There is no such man."

"That's a good attitude to take. It saves face and keeps you from having to do anything. Of course, you feel stupid when the facts come out."

"What facts?"

"Send your niece back."

"What?"

"I can talk to her. I can't talk to you."

"You *cannot* talk to her."

"As you like." Dennis turned back to the bar and picked up his drink.

Minami glared at him for a moment, then went back to her table.

Michiko, without waiting for her, was cutting into the prime rib.

"Stay away from that man."

"Why?"

"He is not a nice man."

"Why, because he likes me?"

"He does not like you. He wants to use you."

"Use me how, Auntie?"

"To get to me."

"What do you mean?"

"You know what I mean. We have to be careful. We are not in our homeland."

Michiko made a face. "Please. When you say things like that, you make it sound like we are in a spy novel."

"We are in a foreign country. We are not speaking in our native tongue. It is not so easy to be clever with words. It is possible to make a slip."

"And wouldn't that be *awful*. If we were to be *embarrassed*. To lose *face*."

"You are rude."

"Oh, pooh." Michiko sawed at her meat. "You just do not want me to have any fun."

"That is not true."

"It is so."

"Do you think it is fun to drink with men in bars?"

"I did not say that."

"What fun are you not having?"

"I am not having *any*. I am just following you around. It is boring."

"You knew it would not be Disney World."

"Oh, pooh." Michiko made a face. "And then you have to pretend to solve a crime."

"I do not pretend."

Michiko pushed a carrot around on her plate. "What do we do tomorrow?"

"I have an interview with a newspaper."

"Oh." The girl rolled her eyes. "Whoopdedo."

From the door to the bar, Dennis Pride watched the two women with interest.

Now how could he make something out of that?

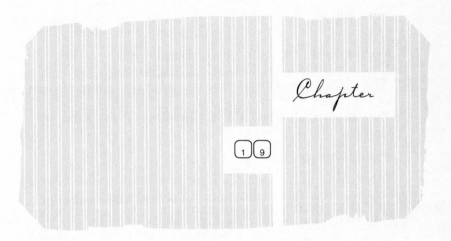

Chapter

1 9

Aaron Grant ran his column though spell-check and hit SEND. He resented doing that. He liked the idea of dropping it on the editor's desk. He kept hoping the e-mail would screw up and make the editor prefer a hard copy. But it never did.

Aaron went out, walked down the street to his car.

Cora was leaning on the hood.

Aaron smiled. "Hi, Cora. What are you doing here? Checking up on your competition?"

"Huh?"

He jerked his thumb. "The Sudoku Lady. She's in there giving an interview."

"You're kidding."

"Freddie's interviewing her about her sudoku books."

"She's up there right now?"

"Yeah. With her niece and some guy. I think he's her agent."

"Zombie in a suit?"

"That's him."

"Well, isn't that interesting?"

"You didn't know about it?"

"No."

Aaron frowned. "So what are you doing here?"

"Oh. I want to talk to you without Sherry."

"That sounds ominous."

"Not at all. You know I'm trying to move out so I won't be underfoot."

"You don't have to do that."

"That's what Sherry says. She's just trying to be polite. Now you're trying to be polite. Everyone's trying to be polite, and nothing gets said. You kids are young. You wanna start a family."

"Who says we want to start a family?"

"Of course you want to start a family. Everyone wants to start a family."

"You never did."

"Yeah, but I'm the exception that proves the rule. It would be easier if Sherry wasn't trying to stop me."

"You want me to persuade Sherry to let you move out?"

"Is that a problem?"

"Sherry's a difficult person to persuade."

"Tell me about it. The point is, if you could ease off urging me to stay, without actually appearing to be siding with me against her—"

"Good God, did you manipulate all your ex-husbands?"

"Come on, wouldn't you like to be rid of me?"

"You kind of grow on people."

"Great." Cora jerked her thumb. "You sure the Sushi Lady isn't up there going through your files?"

"I thought it was Sudoku Lady."

"I know what it is. Is she doing it?"

"Why would she be?"

"See what you've got on Steve Preston."

"What about Steve Preston?"

"He appears to have had a relationship with the deceased."

"You're kidding."

"You didn't have that either? Wow, it's great to be ahead of everybody. Except Dennis, of course."

"What?"

"Yeah. Good news. He's not poking around Sherry. He's poking around the crime."

"Who's the witness?"

"Promise you won't write it?"

"Write it? It sounds like fifth-hand information. Damn it, what's Dennis still doing in town?"

"Talk to his lawyer. On second thought, that's not such a good idea either. Anyway, I'd like to know if Dennis tipped our Japanese friend off. That's assuming he didn't follow her in the first place. Which I would not like at all, because it would mean she was ahead of me. Bad enough it's just Dennis."

Aaron looked at her suspiciously. "You're always keeping me away from Dennis. Now you're throwing him in my face. Why?"

"No reason. But you might pay me back for the heads-up."

"What do you mean?"

"I'd kind of like to know if Sudoku-face is being interviewed or going through the files on Mrs. Fielding's lover."

"Did you follow her here? Was the whole wanting-to-talk-to-me-about-moving-out bit just a ruse?"

"Not at all. It's a legitimate concern. But as a reporter, aren't you interested in whether Minami is actually up there doing research?"

Aaron exhaled sharply, turned, and stalked off back to the paper.

He was out in five minutes.

"Well?" Cora said.

"She's in Freddie's office. She's doing the interview. She isn't going through the files."

"Oh."

Aaron cocked his head.

"Her niece is."

"Really?"

"It doesn't have to mean anything. She's probably just a nosy teenager."

"Yeah, maybe. Where's Zombie Agent?"

"Sitting in on the interview. I get the impression he's trying to run things."

Cora grimaced. "That can't be good."

Aaron shrugged. "Come on. How could it possibly matter?"

Chapter

2 0

DUELING DETECTIVES:
THE SUDOKU LADY VS. THE PUZZLE LADY

Underneath the banner headline in the *Bakerhaven Gazette* were
two pictures: Minami in full geisha regalia, and Cora Felton holding up a box of Granville Grains Post Toasties.

The Sudoku Lady versus the Puzzle Lady? It sounds like a comic
book, but it might be a reality. Minami, the internationally famous Sudoku Lady, has come all the way from Japan to challenge Cora Felton, Bakerhaven's own Puzzle Lady, to a duel.

Charming, polite, and respectful, Minami had nothing but
kind words for her American counterpart, but her agent, Irving
Swartzman, was less reticent. "Minami is not some American

ripoff. She's the real deal. A genuine Japanese Sudoku Lady. Always has been. Always will be. Not some crossword puzzle person who hopped on the sudoku bandwagon when it became hot."

Harsh words but not without a grain of truth. Cora Felton is admittedly a newcomer to the sudoku game. And why should this matter? The demure Sudoku Lady was reluctant to say, but as Mr. Swartzman pointed out, "Crime is mathematical. A person good with numbers is apt to be good at crime. In her own country Minami is often called in to assist the police. She could do the same here, if they were smart enough to ask her."

Even without police cooperation, Swartzman insists, the Sudoku Lady could beat the Puzzle Lady hands down. In fact, while he could not talk about it, Mr. Swartzman hinted that the Sudoku Lady might have some opinions about an ongoing investigation. "Mark my words. The Sudoku Lady is going to solve a crime before the Puzzle Lady. And that's a promise."

Will the challenge be taken up? Only time will tell.

The Puzzle Lady could not be reached for comment.

Chief Harper lowered the paper and cocked his head at Cora. "Would you care to comment?"

"Bite me."

"Let me get this straight. This is all because on a given Sunday your book sold more than her book on the Japanese best-seller list?"

"I don't think you actually *sell* books on a list. I think it's the books that are *sold* that get you *on* it."

"You know what I mean. Stop changing the subject. The point is, this woman is making trouble because of you."

"If you want to look at it that way."

"How else can I look at it?"

"I would say you're lucky she didn't plant a sudoku at the scene of the crime so she could solve it and show you how smart she was."

"That's absurd."

"Is it? How about her body-in-the-freezer theory? Short of mystery books, you're not going to find that one."

"That's different."

"Why?"

"Well, there's nothing Japanese about it."

"There's nothing Japanese about sudoku, either. They didn't invent 'em, they just took 'em over."

"You sound angry."

"Of course, I'm angry. Here's this woman stirring up trouble where there's none, challenging me to prove there's none. Was there ever anything so unfair? Now I got Dennis sticking his nose in—a coincidental lover that had nothing to do with what is actually an accidental trip-and-fall, but that woman's going to make a big deal of it."

"It's not your problem."

"Of course it's my problem. The woman called me out. Am I supposed to get on my high horse, say, 'Don't be silly, I don't wanna play?'"

"That would seem like the thing to do."

"Yeah, if I want my book sales to plummet in Japan."

"You're worried about your book sales?"

"I'm not worried about my book sales. I think it's unfair that a woman comes halfway around the world to screw with my book sales."

"This Steve Preston."

"What about him?"

"You talk to his wife?"

Cora's eyes widened. "Why do you say that?"

"Well, one theory is he killed Mrs. Fielding to keep her from telling his wife. Another would be his wife found out and killed her rival. Actually a simpler motive."

"A simple-*minded* motive. Of a convoluted crime."

"You just called this a convoluted crime."

"So?"

"If it's an accidental death, there's no crime."

"So what?"

"So you started thinking of it as a crime."

"I misspoke."

"That's unusual for a wordsmith who contorts words into intricate constructions seldom heard in the annals of English history."

Cora contorted some words into intricate constructions that George Carlin couldn't say on TV.

Chief Harper went to the file cabinet, jerked it open, and pulled out a file. "You see this?" He pointed to the word stamped on the side. "C-L-O-S-E-D. CLOSED. This is Mrs. Fielding's file. It's closed. It's got nothing to do with you. You got nothing to do with it."

"What if Sally Sudoku comes to me with a theory?"

"Take it to Chief Harper. That's what you tell her. Tell her to bring it to me. You got nothing to do with the case—she should bring it to me."

"And if she doesn't like that answer and rips out my heart with a mat knife?"

"I'll arrest her. Your life will be avenged."

"Somehow I find that small consolation."

"Okay, tell her you got a better theory, and then prove it."

Cora grimaced. "I was afraid you'd say that."

Cora knew Sheila Preston. At least she knew her by sight. Sheila
Preston was one of the young professional wives who hung out in
Cushman's Bake Shop early in the morning before heading off to
their appointed careers. Sheila's was in marketing. Low-level marketing. Entry-level, actually. She was a cashier at Wal-Mart.

Aaron had once done a feature on Sheila Preston, not on her
specifically but on a group of women's annual pledge drive for
public radio. Cora, who hated pledge drives, had refused to par-
ticipate, only one in a long line of charitable causes for which her
celebrity status had attracted unwelcome solicitations.

Armed with the newspaper clipping for identification, Cora
drove out to the mall to accost the young woman on her lunch
hour.

She wasn't there, neither among the cashiers at the registers nor those lunching in the lounge. Cora hunted up the manager, a stocky man with a rather self-satisfied smile.

"Nope, not here."

"I can see that. Where is she?"

"She got laid off. Almost three weeks now."

"How come?"

"Not my place to say."

"You're the manager. Whose place is it?"

"I mean it wouldn't be right for me to comment on an employee's performance."

"Suppose I was thinking about hiring her?"

"Are you?"

"Let's say I am?"

"Where and at what?"

"At Kmart."

"You don't work for Kmart."

"What gave me away?"

"If you want to know why she left, why don't you ask her yourself?"

"I would, but she's not here. Where is she?"

He shrugged. "If she hasn't gotten another job, she's probably home."

"Where's home?"

"I'm not at liberty to say."

"Who is?"

"Beats me." He shrugged again. "I imagine it's in the phone book."

It was. Sheila Preston lived on a pleasant tree-lined street on the edge of town in a two-story wood-frame house on a block of such structures. There was a car parked in the driveway and another car out front, which was good in that she was probably home and bad in that someone was probably with her. Cora pulled up to the curb halfway down the street and cut the motor.

The front door burst open.

A flurry of silk emerged, whirled in multicolored swirls as if doubling back, then glided down the front path to the car, wrenched the door open, hopped in, and took off.

Well, that was interesting. Why was Minami fleeing from Sheila's house? Why had she turned back? Why had she changed her mind? And what the devil had lit such a fire under her in the first place?

Cora considered her options. One was to chase after Minami and see where she went. The other was to call Chief Harper and tell him what the woman had done.

Yeah, right.

Cora got out of her car, walked down the street to the house, went up on the porch, and rang the bell. She could hear it ring inside the house. It was loud. No way the woman couldn't hear. But there was no answer.

Cora noticed the front door was open a crack. That must have been why Minami turned back. To close the door. Only she hadn't. It was clearly open. Unless the lock was off-kilter and there was just an unusual gap.

Cora pushed on the door.

It swung open.

Uh oh.

Cora stuck her head in and called, "Mrs. Preston?"

There was no answer.

Cora slipped through the front door, found herself in a small foyer with a living room off to the left, a kitchen off to the right, and a stairway to the second floor.

Cora went into the living room.

Mrs. Preston lay in the hearth.

Her head had been bashed in, but not by falling on the and-iron. She'd been hit with a poker. It lay next to the body.

There was a piece of paper under the poker.

A sudoku.

				8	3			6
3				4				
	4			6		5		8
		4					5	
	3	6		9				
								2
	2		9					3
			1			7	9	
				5				1

Cora whipped out her cell phone and called Chief Harper. "Chief, it's Cora. I just found Sheila Preston, dead. Come and take charge."

At least that was the fantasy that raced through her head as she stood there. The chance of it happening was slim. For one thing, Cora didn't have a cell phone. For another, calling the police, though the right and proper thing to do, was not high on her list of options.

Cora took a quick look around to make sure that in addition to the sudoku there wasn't any damn crossword puzzle. She found none.

Okay. Good. Now let's make sense of the scene. Minami comes to interview the woman and . . .

Panics and runs away?

Nonsense. Why would she do that? She got freaked out by the sudoku? No way. She's the Sudoku Lady. She *expects* a sudoku. The killer's bound to leave her one.

So why hightail it out of there? Why not call the cops? What is it about the sudoku . . . ?

Cora stopped.

Her mouth fell open.

Minami calls on the woman, finds her dead.

There *is* no sudoku.

Minami *plants* a sudoku. To make herself important. To make it appear that the killer is taunting her. To involve herself in the investigation of the crime.

In which case, she doesn't want to discover the body. She wants someone *else* to discover the body.

Cora was damned if it was going to be her.

She glanced around. Was there anything she hadn't noticed? No. Was there anything she'd touched? Just the door. No problem there. She'd have to touch the door. She could leave.

Except . . .

Was the woman dead?

That was rather major. She should make sure that she's dead. How could she do that? Give her another whack with the poker? Old joke. Feel her pulse?

Pulse, hell. She's dead as a doorknob.

The one she touched.

God, she was losing it.

Get out, get out, get out.

Cora came out the front door, hurried down the walk. Saw no one. Slipped into her car.

Okay, now what?

Drive to the police station, get Chief Harper. No. That was as bad as finding the body. *Telling* him she found the body. Worse. She should have *stayed* with the body. No, what she needed was someone *else* to find the body. A neighbor, maybe. Let's see. How could she motivate a neighbor?

The direct approach. Bang on a neighbor's door. Say she'd been ringing the doorbell and getting no answer, but the woman had to be there because her car was there, and did the neighbor see her go out? Get the neighbor interested. Talk the neighbor into coming with her. Let the neighbor discover the door was ajar. "How stupid of me, I should have noticed. Do you think we should go in?" Let the neighbor go first, find the body, freak out. Keep the neighbor from touching anything, wrestle her outside, make her go back to her house and call the police.

Cora grimaced. Harper wouldn't buy it. Harper would know she was pulling a fast one.

Harper would think *she* planted the damn sudoku.

While Cora was wrestling with her conscience, a black rental car pulled up and stopped in front of the house.

Dennis Pride got out.

Cora's mouth fell open. Jesus Christ. Someone was coming to find the body. But it was the last person in the world she wanted. What would Dennis do? Call the cops? Not likely. Steal the sudoku? Wipe the poker? Even Dennis wasn't that crazy. Unless he committed the crime himself, there was no one he'd care enough to protect. Except Sherry. And Sherry had nothing to do with it. Dennis must know that.

Dennis looked up and down the street.

Cora ducked behind the steering wheel. Had he recognized

her car? She risked a glance. After all, if he'd seen her, the jig was up.

But he hadn't. Dennis was on his way up the walk. He reached the front door, rang the bell. Waited a while, rang again.

Uh oh.

Dennis spotted the door.

Pushed it open, slipped inside.

He was back in a minute, as freaked out as Cora had ever seen him. He glanced around, practically sprinted down the walk, hopped in his car, and sped off.

Well, it was a cinch *he* wasn't going to call the cops.

Back to square one. Dead body. No witness.

So what now? Should she phone in an anonymous tip?

A car came down the street. What was this—Grand Central Station? If it was someone else calling on Mrs. Preston, Cora was going to lose it.

Sure enough, the car stopped right in front of her house.

Michiko got out, sullen as ever in her T-shirt and jeans. Minami followed and, flapping silk sleeves like a giant moth, herded her teenage niece up the walk and in the front door.

The two women were out moments later, Michiko looking slightly less bored. She whipped a cell phone out of her jeans.

Cora didn't wait to see who the girl called. She slipped the Toyota into gear and sped off.

A minute and a half later she screeched to a stop in front of the police station.

Chief Harper was coming out the door.

Cora rolled down the window. "Hey, Chief!"

Harper waved her off. "Not now! There's been another one!"

"Oh?"

Harper hopped in the cruiser and took off. Cora was right behind.

With his lights and siren, Chief Harper made it to Mrs. Preston's house in just slightly more time than it had taken Cora to come from it.

Minami and Michiko were huddled out front.

"Okay, where is it?" Harper barked.

Minami pointed up the path.

"All right. Officers are on the way. You stay here, don't talk to anyone until I get back." As Cora came bustling up, he added, "Particularly her."

"What happened?" Cora said.

Minami set her lips, raised her chin.

Her niece's eyes were wide. "There's a dead woman in there!"

"Michiko!"

"Well, there is."

"Did you not hear the policeman? He said not to talk."

"Of course," Cora said. "And that's exactly what your lawyer will tell you."

"Lawyer!" Minami said.

"Yes, of course. Anyone finding a dead body is a natural suspect. Especially when the police have no one else to arrest. They probably don't. Unless it's a domestic thing. Who is it—the housewife?" Cora grimaced. "I hate to promote the stereotype. The fact is, there's a lot of housewives. It's the first thing you think of. Not the househusband."

"It's her."

"Michiko!"

"Wow. That must be something. You ever see a dead body before?"

Minami put herself in front of Michiko. "I will thank you not to question my niece. The policeman has told us not to talk. You are trying to make her disobey. You will get her into trouble."

Chief Harper came back out. "Well, you were right to call the police. Did you touch anything?"

"No." Minami pointed a finger accusingly. "This woman has been trying to talk to my niece."

"Tattletale."

"After you said not to. My niece is young. Impressionable. It is not right. It is not honorable."

Cora shrugged. "I never claimed to be as honorable as you. I just have better book sales."

Harper gave her a glance.

Cora put up her hands. "All right, all right, I'll be good. But what do you mean telling these women not to talk? Is there some sort of conspiracy of silence? It seems unlike your police department."

Harper ignored her and said to Minami, "Tell me what happened."

"You wish me to speak in front of her?"

"As Miss Felton has pointed out, the police have nothing to hide. Go ahead."

Before Minami could answer, a hatchet-faced woman from the house across the street came walking up. "Is something wrong?"

Harper exhaled in exasperation, and looked around for his officers. Neither of them were there yet. "Cora, you want to handle crowd control until Dan and Sam get here?"

Cora put up her hands. "Sorry, Chief, I'm afraid I'm not authorized to do that."

"Something happened, didn't it?" the woman said. "I almost called you myself."

"And why is that?" Chief Harper said.

The hatchet-faced woman pointed at Minami. "I looked out my window and saw this woman running away from the house." She nodded in agreement with herself. "I'm surprised she came back."

Cora's heart stopped. Of all the bad things in the world that could have happened, this was the worst. Yeah, it was nice to see Minami get her comeuppance. But not like this. Not with an eyewitness. Not with one who saw her fleeing the house.

It wasn't just that Cora felt compassion for the woman. The icy dread that gripped her was not for her Japanese rival. No, it was the realization that if the nosy neighbor had seen that, there were other things she might have seen.

Like Cora. Or Dennis. Or the actual murderer.

Cora wouldn't have minded the actual murderer much. It would have made for a dull and simple crime. Still, clearing the main participants of murder would be sufficient compensation.

Good lord. She sounded like a walking thesaurus. Come on.

Time to slip into gun-moll mode. You're about to be arrested for a crime.

But she wasn't.

The hatchet-faced busybody from across the street, Mrs. Thelma Wilson, was saying, "I went in the kitchen, and I was thinking I should call the police, and then the water boiled, and I was making tea and ramen noodles, so convenient, since they both need boiling water. And then when I had my lunch made, I wanted to eat it while it was hot, and by the time I got back to the window, you were already here."

Cora exhaled in relief. So, she was off the hook and Minami was on it, and all was right with the world.

Cora immediately switched gears and prepared to align herself with the officers of the law in the swift execution of their solemn duty.

"You're sure this is the woman you saw coming out of the house?" Harper said.

"That's right."

"Perhaps you'd care to tell us what you were doing the *first* time you called on the woman," Chief Harper said dryly. "When you came to see her, was she already dead? Or did she open the door and let you in?"

"Aunt Minami! What is he saying? Tell him you didn't do that!"

"Sorry," Harper said, "but it looks like she did. And you're not supposed to do that. It's called failing to report a crime."

Minami clamped her lips together.

"Go ahead and tell him," Cora said.

Minami glared at her.

So did Michiko.

Chief Harper looked at her in surprise.

"Tell him everything you did. Everything you can think of. Don't leave anything out. Tell him every little detail."

In spite of herself, Minami couldn't help asking, "Why?"

"He now suspects you of a crime. He just said so. And he hasn't informed you of your rights. Nothing you say can be used in evidence against you. It's all inadmissible. He can't get you for anything."

Harper's mouth fell open. He whirled on Cora, his face red with rage.

A police car screeched to a stop. Sam Brogan got out, his laconic manner in stark contrast to the speed of the vehicle. "What have we got here?" he drawled.

"Crime scene. Check it out."

Sam popped his gum, wandered off.

Harper turned back to Minami. "You're under arrest on suspicion of being an accessory to murder. You have the right to remain silent . . ."

Cora turned to Michiko. "Got a cell phone?"

"Why?"

"Call information. Ask for the number of Becky Baldwin."

Chapter

24

Becky Baldwin came down the front steps of the police station.

Cora was waiting to pounce. "I thought you'd never come out."

"I was talking to my client."

"Without me."

"It was a confidential conversation with my client."

"Exactly. That's why I wanted to be there."

"I can't let you do that."

"You've done it before."

"I've never had a client who was in direct competition with you before."

"That's just stupid."

"Tell *her* about it. I suggested you might be of help, but she declined the offer. I pointed out that I'd often hired you as a private investigator. She claims she doesn't need a private investigator. She's a better investigator than you are, and she can't wait to show you up."

"Oh, for goodness' sake. Does the woman realize she's charged with murder?"

"I tried to impress it on her. She didn't seem particularly concerned."

"Of course not. She's stoic. It's a cultural thing. What does she say about the murder?"

"She knows nothing about the murder. Someone's clearly trying to frame her."

"With the sudoku?"

Becky frowned. "I'm afraid I can't get into the specifics."

Cora was astounded. "What?"

"I can't discuss my client's case with you."

"I got you the job!"

"I'm grateful. But my primary duty is to my client."

"Go ahead and do it. No one's stopping you. I fail to see how filling me in on the situation would make the slightest difference."

"I can't really tell you that without filling you in on the situation."

"You want me to pull your hair out?"

"I'd rather you didn't."

"Becky, it's me, Cora. You think I'll tell I'll tell you told? I'll go to the grave rather than rat you out. Tell me what she said and I'll tell you if it's true."

"You'll just get me in trouble."

"I promise I won't let it slip."

"That's what you think. When you're on a case, nothing can stop you. You might not *say* anything, but if you started investigating something as a result of something I told you that you couldn't have learned from any other source, it would be a dead giveaway. She'd know I told you, and there'd be hell to pay."

"You're afraid I'll get you fired?"

"I'm afraid you'll get me *disbarred*. This is one headstrong woman who wants her own way." Becky shrugged. "I know, what a bizarre concept."

"Watch it."

"Anyway, the woman has chosen to confide in me. It was a confidential communication and bound by attorney-client privilege. If it hadn't been, she wouldn't have made it. But she did and I have to respect it."

"Good lord, what's the trouble? Is she guilty?"

"Of course not. My clients are never guilty. It's absurd. She came all the way from Japan to kill a woman she never met?"

"I think there's a Western like that."

"I'm sure there is. Anyway, thanks for the recommendation. I need the work. Sorry I can't tell you anything, but that's the way it goes." Becky cocked her head. "So, are you free to investigate?"

Cora's mouth fell open. "Are you kidding me?"

"It's a serious charge. I intend to take every precaution."

"You want me to work for you and you won't tell me why?"

"You know why. To get a woman out of jail."

"You gonna tell her you're hiring me?"

"It's none of her business."

"You're gonna pass the bills along to her, aren't you?"

"Well, I'm not going to pay you myself."

"If she's so snooty about her own detective skills, won't she object?"

Becky smiled. "Not if she doesn't know."

Cora shook her head. "I'm going to kill you before this is over."

"I don't hold a grudge. I'll defend you of the charge."

"That's nice of you. Okay, if I'm going to work for you, there's some things I need to know. Why did your client come back to see the body again?"

"I can't answer that."

"Did your client plant a sudoku next to the body?"

"I can't answer that."

"That's as good as an admission."

"No, it isn't."

"If she didn't, you could just deny it."

"I can't and you know it. Then you could cherry-pick. Anything I didn't deny, you'd know was true."

"You're not denying she planted the sudoku, even though she didn't?"

"I can't answer that."

"This is a hell of a situation."

"Isn't it?" Becky cocked her head. "So, you want the job?"

Chief Harper wasn't pleased to see Cora. "You've got a lot of nerve."

"What do you mean?"

"Walking in here just like that."

"How do you want me to walk in?"

"Don't be cute. You sold me out. Undercut my interrogation, told a suspect I was doing it wrong, and made me look like a fool."

"Oh, come on, Chief. I don't think you looked like that much of a fool."

"You got my suspect to clam up and call a lawyer."

"Well, Becky needed the work."

"It's not funny, Cora. This was a very simple situation. All the woman had to do was explain. Instead, I got her in a holding cell,

Becky Baldwin's demanding her release, and Henry Firth is running around trying to figure how many things he can charge her with."

"Tell Ratface to calm down."

"Will you stop calling him Ratface?"

"Well, tell him to stop poking his ratty nose in where it isn't wanted. For a prosecutor, the guy's a real busybody."

"You should talk."

"Chief!"

"I'm sorry, Cora, but you give the woman advice like that. 'Tell the chief anything you want; he's so bad at procedure he won't be able to get you on it.'"

"That's not exactly how I phrased it."

"That was the gist. What the hell were you doing?"

"Come on, Chief. The woman was about to make a few evasive answers and walk out. Then you'd have nothing. Instead, she clams up and calls a lawyer and you got a suspect in jail."

"But she didn't do it!"

"Big deal. By the time she talks you'll get the one who actually did do it, and everyone will be so pleased you arrested him, no one will care you arrested her."

"That whole argument would sound more plausible if you weren't competing on the best-seller list."

"That's cynical, even for you, Chief. Come on, whaddya got?"

"I got nothing."

"You got the woman in jail. What's her story?"

"Becky won't let her talk. Thanks to you. I ought to put *you* in jail."

"On what charge?"

"Obstructing a police investigation."

"Don't be silly. I'm here to *help* you with the police investigation."

"You could have helped me by keeping quiet in the first place."

"The woman's not stupid. I don't like her, but she's not stupid. She got caught with egg on her face. There were only two possibilities: There's a simple explanation for what she did or there isn't. If there's a simple explanation, she's gonna make it. It doesn't matter what you say or I say or the neighbor says. She's gonna say something like, 'When I have a severe emotional shock, I get flustered and I can't speak English, my thoughts are all in Japanese, and I need to talk to someone Japanese in order to snap me out of it.' "

At Harper's rather impatient look, Cora put up her hand. "Granted, that's not a great example. I'm spitballing this off the top of my head. But the point is, if the explanation was that simple, that logical, that straightforward, and that unincriminating, she'd come out with it. Or even if she consulted a lawyer, her *lawyer* would come out with it. But that didn't happen here. By forcing her hand, you've got her lawyer stonewalling, and you know something's up. Which puts you at a tremendous advantage. You're not the mean old police chief harassing a poor helpless woman— you're the guy who asked a perfectly reasonable question and is waiting patiently for an answer in the face of an inexplicably elaborate stonewall."

Harper grumbled and shook his head. "You make it sound so logical."

"That's only because it is, Chief. Now, in terms of the crime. You got a time of death yet?"

"We're not working together."

"I'm glad to hear it. That would seem like collusion. Particularly when I'm working for the other side."

"Becky Baldwin hired you?"

"Shhh! Hey, don't tell anyone. Her client would be pissed."

"You're working for Becky Baldwin and you're here trying to pump me for information for the defense?"

"Don't be silly. We're on the same side. We want to catch the killer, whoever he or she may be. Notice I said or she, so as not to exempt the person currently behind bars. So, what do the facts show? Obviously nothing in the woman's favor. If the evidence cleared her, you wouldn't be in the embarrassing position of having to substantiate the charge."

"It's not embarrassing if she happens to be guilty."

"Oh, come on, Chief. On your list of potential murder suspects, I would think a woman from Japan who didn't know the victim would be pretty close to the bottom. Wouldn't the *husband* be a slightly better prospect?"

"Steve Preston was at work in Manhattan at the time of the crime."

"I thought you didn't *know* the time of the crime."

"No, I just evaded the question. Barney hasn't pinned it down, but we know generally."

"So what is it?"

"I'm going to have to evade again."

"And you call *me* annoying."

"You *are* annoying. You're a defense investigator, for goodness' sake, and I'm letting you stay. What are you griping about?"

Cora sighed, took out her cigarettes. "I don't know. I'm in a bad mood. I don't have a man. I gotta move out."

"And you can't smoke."

"Oh, lash the dog!"

"You're lucky I don't confiscate your cigarettes."

"You're not helping with my bad mood. Where was I? No

house, no man. Oh, yes, we're in a recession. Times are tough. On top of everything else, my ex-husbands could get wiped out. What would I do then?"

Cora tapped a cigarette from the pack and took out her lighter.

"You light that, I'll throw you in jail."

Cora flicked the lighter defiantly. Stopped. Blew it out. "Say, there's an idea."

Harper frowned. "What?"

Cora smiled brightly. "Arrest me!"

The steel door of the holding cell clanged shut.

Cora put her hands on the bars and yelled, "You'll never hold me, copper!"

Chief Harper smiled grimly and went out, closing the door behind him.

Cora sat on the cot, side-spied at Minami in the adjoining cell. "What are you in for, sister?"

Minami stuck her nose in the air. "You think you are funny."

"I know I'm funny. I'm a female Groucho Marx." Cora winced. "Just dated myself again. You probably never heard of him. Trust me, I'm hilarious."

"You are trying to get me to talk. You are, how do you say, a pigeon on a stool."

"A stool pigeon."

"That is the bird. It is not nice, and it will not work. Pretending to be put in jail so I will confide in you. Did you think I would fall for so obvious a trick? Call your police friend. Have him let you out."

"I would, but he can't hear."

"What?"

"The door is soundproofed. For the drunks. When they arrest a drunk, they don't want to hear him all night."

"Then give the signal."

"What signal?"

"Do you not wear a wire? A hidden microphone? A recording device?"

"You're clearly unfamiliar with the budget of the Bakerhaven Police Department. The only thing they ever record is Christmas carols on Dan Finley's iPod."

"I do not understand."

"Just as well. There's no wire, microphone, intercom, buzzer, or any other communication device with which to signal the chief. When he locks you up, you're here until he comes back." Cora cocked her head. "Did he give you the puzzle?"

Minami said nothing and looked away.

"He didn't give you the puzzle? He gave me the puzzle. But he wouldn't give me a pencil. Afraid I might stab somebody. So I have to solve it from memory. Wanna help?"

"I am not talking to you."

"I noticed." Cora took out the sudoku. "Wanna look at it? It looks tough but not impossible. Not what you would call diabolical. Actually, I don't know what you'd call it. I haven't read your books."

Minami maintained a dignified silence.

"Of course you haven't read mine. Why should you? Who

cares, anyway? Just a bunch of damn numbers. Of course, choosing the *right* numbers, that's an art. Making it just good enough to be fun. Took me a while to get that. Solving is easy. Constructing is a bitch." Cora shrugged. "Aw, what do you care? You don't. It's just a lousy sudoku. Except . . . it's with a dead body. That makes it interesting. Is it a clue? If so, what does it mean? Who left it? You wouldn't expect the killer to leave something to implicate him. Or her. Or it. You know, in case she was killed by an asexual Martian robot."

Cora waited for a response but got none. Shrugged. "Huh. Might as well be talking to the wall." She studied the puzzle. "I don't know why you're not interested in this sudoku."

"It is stupid. It means nothing. It is a fish that is red."

"A red herring."

"That is the one. That is what it must be."

"And why would the killer put it there?"

"Because it is a very simple crime. If there was no sudoku, you would know who did it. So there is a sudoku, so you will not."

"You're pretty smart. Even if you're not that good of a crook. You may have experience with crime, but I bet it's always been solving it. Committing it is a whole other proposition. Frankly, you're just no good."

Minami refused to be baited.

"Where you fall down is finding the body twice. Big mistake. Finding the body once is bad enough. But a second time? It's an amateur move and you hate to see it. If anyone sees you the first time, it undercuts the second. The next thing you know you're in a jail cell with little chance of escape. None, actually, if your lawyer won't let you talk. Then your situation does not change and you're here for the duration. That means the end, and there is no end in sight. And I can't see staying here for it. Just overnight would be bad enough." Cora patted the cot. "Imagine sleeping on one of these things? Barely wide enough. Good thing I don't have to. I called my lawyer. I'll be bailed out soon. You've already seen your lawyer, right? And it didn't work. You're still here. What a shame."

"Please stop. You make no sense."

"I just can't figure out why you'd go back. The police think it was to plant the sudoku. But why would you do that? I can't buy it. The risk is too great, the reward too small.

"Unless you *had* to go back. Unless you left something there you'd forgotten. But how could you forget? It's a crime scene. You're on your guard. For every least little thing. You'd have to be really flustered to forget something. But you do. You go away. You come back with your niece." Cora's eyes widened. "Your niece. You go get your niece, and she tells you something and you have to go back. What could she know? Was *she* there before?"

"That is just stupid."

"Is it? It clearly bothers you. Like I struck a nerve. How could your niece be involved? She didn't know him. He had no connection . . . Oh, my God!"

"What?"

"Nothing."

"You said, 'Oh, my God!'"

"I did. Maybe it was a ploy to get you to talk."

"If it was, you would not tell me it was."

"Don't count on it. I'm tricky."

"Why did you say, 'Oh, my God!'?"

"You're interested. You think I said 'Oh, my God!' about your niece and you're interested. Has your niece met anyone lately?"

"You're impertinent."

"I am not the one buying her sexy jeans. Has your niece made any new friends?"

"I am not talking to you."

"Unless it suits your purpose," Cora observed.

"My lawyer said not to talk."

"I'm sure she did. Smart girl, that Becky. So, your niece had some interest in the crime scene."

"I am not talking to you."

"I wonder what it was."

Minami said nothing.

"Maybe Chief Harper can find out." Cora sighed and then said into the microphone, "Okay, Chief, let me out."

Becky Baldwin was adamant. "I can't let you talk to her."

"Why not?"

"I'm her attorney."

"You can't be everyone's attorney. You're Minami's attorney. You're Dennis Pride's attorney. You can't be Michiko's attorney, too."

"Why not?"

"It's a conflict of interest."

"Not at all. Michiko's interests are the same as her aunt's."

"You're saying if Minami's convicted of murder, Michiko should take the fall, too?"

"Don't be silly. Minami didn't murder anyone."

"Then why is she in jail?"

"The police made a mistake."

"You blame Chief Harper?"

"Not entirely."

"You blame me?"

"I don't blame you."

"I'm glad to hear it."

"The whole thing is a terrible misunderstanding."

"So everyone can apologize and Minami can go home?"

"You can be really annoying when you want to."

"I don't want to be annoying. I just want to talk to little Miss Jailbait."

"That's hardly the way to curry favor."

"Come on, Becky. You don't really think the girl did it, and I don't really think the girl did it. But she may have information that would be helpful."

"What makes you think that?"

"Her sexy jeans."

"Huh?"

"She's just the type of nymphet to appeal to a certain type of predator. If there was any young man around with a notorious lack of moral character—"

"Excuse me?"

"I don't mean to point any fingers, but you have a client who would seem to match that description."

"You mean Dennis?"

"Is it that obvious? You better be nice to me, or I'll tell him you got it in one guess. Of course, you do have a rather short client list."

Becky looked at Cora narrowly. "I'm really ticking you off, aren't I? You're not usually quite so caustic."

"I'm not usually dealing with the inscrutable Japanese." Cora frowned. "Or is it the Chinese that are inscrutable? I have to watch my political incorrectness. Anyway, I'm wondering if Dennis has taken an interest in the niece."

"Why are you wondering that?"

Cora cocked her head. "You know, if we were leveling with each other, I'd be inclined to share that information with you. But since we're dealing at arm's length—"

"I've told you all I can."

"Fine. Now, let her tell me all *she* can. How about I talk to her in your presence? You could tell her what questions to answer."

Becky considered the proposition. "Not at the moment."

"Okay, back to the drawing board. Wanna see the sudoku?"

"You have the sudoku?"

"Harper gave it to me. Wanna see it?"

"Sure."

Cora dug the sudoku out of her purse.

Becky unfolded it and took a look.

9	5	2	7	8	3	4	1	6
3	6	8	5	4	1	9	2	7
7	4	1	2	6	9	5	3	8
2	7	4	3	1	6	8	5	9
5	3	6	8	9	2	1	7	4
8	1	9	4	5	7	3	6	2
1	2	5	9	7	8	6	4	3
6	8	3	1	2	4	7	9	5
4	9	7	6	3	5	2	8	1

Cora jerked her thumb at the sudoku.

"You hadn't seen it yet?"

"No."

"You didn't demand a copy?"

"Why?"

"For your client to solve."

"What good would that do?"

"I don't know, but it's the logical move."

"Why?"

"What do you mean, why? That's what you do with sudoku. You solve 'em."

"Yes. And whaddya got? A bunch of numbers."

"You don't think it's important?"

"Of course, I think it's important. It's an attempt to frame my client."

"I mean in and of itself."

"No, you don't. You mean the solution. I don't think the solution is important. It's just a bunch of numbers. The importance of the sudoku is that it's a sudoku."

"You think someone left it there to implicate your client?"

"Or to implicate you."

"What?"

"You're a sudoku expert. You've got your own set of books."

"In *Japan*. No one connects me with sudoku here. Not in my column. Not on TV."

"Yeah, but locally—"

"Locally, smocally. People know I can do sudoku. That doesn't mean they're gonna leave 'em lying around for me. Any more than they're gonna leave me a pack of Camel filters or a stray husband. The sudoku doesn't point to me in any way whatsoever. Much as you might like it to."

"Did I say that?"

"No, but I know what you're like when you've got a client. Everyone else in the world is guilty."

"Except my other clients."

"Right. In a perfect world everyone would be your client and there'd be no crime. You're not gonna let me talk to the girl?"

"No."

"Okay, I won't."

Michiko picked at a french fry. "I'm not supposed to talk to you."

"Your lawyer said it was all right."

"Are you sure? She said no one."

"Becky and I go way back. Besides, I bet you talked to someone already."

Michiko's eyes shifted. "What do you mean?"

"A pretty girl like you. I bet you got a lot of admirers."

"Don't be silly."

"Why is that silly?"

"I am a stranger here. I don't know anyone."

"You are pretty. Men will talk to you."

"I am always with my aunt."

"Always? That doesn't seem fair."

"No, but it is the deal."

"Deal?"

"I can go to America if I do what she says. Is that fair?"

"I'm sure you think it isn't."

"How would you like it if you had someone looking after you? Keeping you out of trouble?"

Cora smiled. She couldn't help thinking how many times her niece Sherry had slipped into that role. "It must be very frustrating. Then to find a dead body."

"I barely got to see it."

"Oh?"

"We had just arrived. Then the police came."

"You hadn't seen it before?"

"What do you mean?"

"You know what I mean. Your aunt found a body. Something about it made her think of you. She went back and got you. Too late. The police were there."

"What are you saying?"

"I'm not saying anything. The police will say a lot. That is why your lawyer wants you to keep quiet. Don't tell them anything when she is not around. You may think you know it all, but you are young. These people are tricky. They will get things out of you."

"No one will get anything out of me."

"I'm glad to hear it. So, you didn't know the body was there?"

"I just told you. I had not seen it."

"I know you did. But someone might have told you it was there."

"You mean my aunt."

"I know she told you. I mean someone else."

"Who?"

Cora smiled. "That is a silly question. I'm not the one who

would know. You're the one who would know. You should not be asking me what you know."

"What you think is wrong. *I* know there is no one. I am asking you to tell me what wrong thing *you* think."

"I think you met a man with long hair."

Michiko's eyes faltered.

"I thought so. What did he tell you?"

"Who?"

Cora shook her head. "No good. Unless you've been seeing a lot of men with long hair. Which I doubt. We're talking about the one with the business suit. And the rental car. And the wife."

"Wife!"

"Yeah. He probably didn't mention her, did he? So covering up for him is not such a hot idea."

"I am not covering up for him."

"But you know him. And you tried to keep his name out of it. Are you trying to tell me he knows nothing about the murders?"

"Of course he knows nothing about the murders."

"Did you ask him?"

"What?"

"Did you talk to him about the murders? Did he tell you what he knows?"

"He knows nothing about the murders."

"Did you ask him about them?"

"Why should I? *I* know nothing about the murders."

"Really? Then why were you looking them up in the files of the *Bakerhaven Gazette*?"

Michiko's hand stopped with a french fry halfway to her mouth. "Are you following me?"

"Of course not."

"But you know what I do. You know who I see."

Cora shrugged. "It's a small town. Everyone knows what you do in a small town."

Michiko frowned, ate the french fry.

"So why'd auntie want you to see the corpse?"

Michiko's eyes narrowed. She peered at Cora suspiciously. "Are you sure my lawyer said you could talk to me?"

"Absolutely. Becky and I are like that."

Michiko cocked her head with the saucy smile of a teenage girl.

"Then ask *her*."

Chapter

2 9

Becky was furious. "You talked to her?"

"Maybe a little."

"After you told me you wouldn't."

"Is that what I said?"

"You know damn well what you said. You said you'd leave her alone."

"Are you saying I broke my promise? That's what it sounds like you're saying. That's the type of fight I used to have with Judy Griswold in fourth grade. I usually won, as I recall."

"It's no joke, Cora. It's an abuse of attorney-client privilege."

"Oh, Michiko is your client now? What has she done?"

"She hasn't done anything."

"Then why are you representing her? Are you so hard up for work you're taking on clients for no particular reason?"

"She's a witness in the case against her aunt. I'm representing her aunt. Ergo—"

"Ergo? You're coming at me with an 'ergo'? Becky, it's me— Cora. I'm on your side. Hell, you hired me for goodness' sake."

"I may have to let you go."

"You can't. You haven't paid me yet. Besides, I haven't given my report."

"Report on what?"

"On information you need to keep your client out of the hoosegow. Now, just because I obtained that information by talking to a relative of your client, which, aside from a spouse, isn't covered by attorney-client privilege. Or am I mistaken?"

"What information did you come up with?"

"I'm not sure I should share it with you. After all, it wasn't obtained in a method you approve of, so you probably aren't going to pay me for it."

"Damn it, Cora—"

"I don't see why we're having a problem. Aside from the you-promised hissy fit you seem determined to throw. Anyway, Michiko appears to know something about the murder she isn't letting on. I throw that out for what it's worth. Your move."

"What do you think she knows?"

"Ah, now you're interested? I will answer that question if you promise not to bawl me out about it."

"Now you want *me* to promise?"

"Only so I can needle you when you break it."

"Oh, hell, just tell me what you know."

"I don't know anything. I have my suspicions."

"About what?"

"Michiko's been hanging out with Dennis Pride. Who, I believe, *is* one of your clients."

"You saw them together?"

"No."

"What makes you think they've been together?"

"She was upset when I told her he was married."

Becky frowned. "Oh."

"Yeah, that seemed a bad sign."

"And just why did you tell her Dennis was married?"

"She's young. Impressionable. I thought she should know."

Becky snorted in disgust. "I'm a lawyer and you're going to give me circular logic? You think she's been seeing Dennis because she reacted when you asked her. And you asked her because you think she's been seeing him?"

Cora took a breath. Sighed. "Okay. I hate to rat anyone out. Even Dennis. But here's the scoop."

Cora told Becky about seeing Dennis go into the victim's house. By the time she was done, Becky's mouth was hanging open.

"Dennis might have killed her?"

"Don't be silly. Dennis never killed anyone."

"But he had the opportunity. He's my reasonable doubt. All I have to do is produce Dennis and Minami's out of jail."

"And Dennis is in it. Isn't there some sort of law about turning in your client? Wouldn't that be a genuine conflict of interest? Maybe you should ask the bar association."

Becky put up her hand. "All right, all right. Why'd you have to tell me this? You put me in a terrible position."

Cora smiled. "Yeah. If I'd known it was going to be this much fun, I'd have told you right off."

"Damn it. I may have to bring in outside counsel."

"That's no good. I suppose they'd want to be paid."

"Cora."

"What's the problem? Dennis is your client. Bring him in and sweat him."

"Right. And who shall I say is accusing him?"

"You don't have to say anything. Just present him with the proposition and see how he squirms."

"Wait a minute. You saw Dennis go into the house?"

"That's right."

"What were you doing there?"

"I refuse to answer on the grounds I'm not your client."

"You *are* my client."

"Not in this."

"Damn it. I gotta get Minami out of jail."

"What's stopping you?"

"Legal ethics."

Cora made a face. "You're a lawyer and you're worried about legal ethics?"

Becky looked at Cora with narrowed eyes. "You're way too glib. Did you go in that house?"

Cora just smiled.

"You went in, didn't you? You went in and found her dead. Was that before or after Dennis went in?"

"Dennis went in? Oh, my God. Do the police know that?"

Becky groaned. "What am I going to do with you?"

Cora shrugged. "Well, you could pay me."

Chapter

30

Cora came out of Becky's office and steamed on past the pizza parlor as if it weren't even there, the tantalizing aroma of chicken, onion, pepperoni, and sausage from the daily special barely registering. She flung herself into the front seat of the Toyota and exhaled as if she had been holding her breath for the past hour.

Good lord! How many balls was she juggling? How many lies was she telling? How many stories was she trying to keep straight? Never mind the basic I'm-the-Puzzle-Lady-but-I-can't-do-puzzles secret, known to Sherry, Aaron, and Dennis but not to Becky or Chief Harper. Setting aside the grand deception and focusing only on the current crimes, she had just admitted to Becky that she had seen Dennis going into the house. She had *refused* to admit to Becky that *she* had gone into the house but *had* admitted to Becky about talking to her client's niece. But she withheld from Becky enlisting Aaron to spy on said niece at the paper—to what end she was not entirely sure, since it was not the sort of thing she needed to keep from Becky. It simply had not come up.

From Chief Harper she was withholding just about everything, a wonderful position to be in with an investigating officer, particularly one she was presumably helping. But she couldn't tell him she had seen Dennis go into the house. She couldn't tell him she had seen Minami go into the house. And she certainly couldn't tell him *she* had gone in the house. All in all, there were a lot of people that Cora couldn't mention had been in the house.

By and large, Cora wasn't doing a hell of a job helping the chief with the crime. All she'd really done was solve a meaningless sudoku. She hadn't done anything to see what the solution meant. Not that it *could* mean anything. In the past, when she'd solved a sudoku, there had been a crossword puzzle along with it, to give some hint as to its meaning, to point her in the right direction, to suggest what numbers in the puzzle were important. In this case, there was nothing. Just a number puzzle to implicate the suspect currently in jail.

It occurred to Cora she was lucky *she* wasn't the suspect currently in jail.

Aside from that, nothing was going particularly right. Two people were dead. They shared a common bond of infidelity, which offered a motive for a crime, but, in that case, a crime of passion, not a cold-blooded, methodical murder-by-numbers affair.

It was all coming down on her. She was getting older. She had no man, no job—at least no real job, one she actually did—and no place to live. Only a room in a honeymoon house that she ought to be out of.

Cora drove up the driveway, parked the car, sat, and stewed.

Maybe she should talk this over with her niece. At least she could be open with Sherry, tell her everything.

Except where Dennis was concerned. That was the joker in the deck. It wasn't fair to a bride on her honeymoon to keep throwing her ex-husband in her face.

No, Cora had to figure this out herself. Not that she wasn't up to the task. It just helped to have people to bounce ideas off.

Cora opened the screen door, let the dog out. He yipped happily, darted around the lawn, and returned for a treat.

"What do you think, Buddy?" Cora said.

In times of stress, Cora had come to talk to the dog, the realization of which had led her to believe she was getting senile or at least dotty in a post-romantic-age way. Which was not the way Cora saw herself. Cora saw herself as the lead character in a noir crime novel or a bodice-ripper or some combination of the two. A young, stronger, sexier Cora Felton needed to swoop in and save the day. Particularly, if Buddy was no help.

"Okay, kid," Cora told the dog, "let's assume for a moment that Minami was not guilty of this crime. Which is a damn good assumption. Because, if she was, it would fly in the face of logic." She frowned. "I'm glad you're a dog. Because I'm not sure what flying in the face of logic looks like, though people seem to say it all the time. Anyway, assume she's innocent. In that case, someone is framing her. Framing her with the sudoku. Which is a pretty clumsy frame, unless they knew she was calling on the woman, and how could they know? But assume they did. Or assume that even if Minami isn't seen going into the house, the presence of the sudoku will call attention to her. She's known to be investigating the crime. Surely, that is enough to establish a link."

Cora looked at the dog. "What do you think, Buddy? Would you assume someone was trying to frame Minami?"

Buddy wagged his tail, spun in a circle, and peed on a bush.

"Right," Cora said, "there's no reason to make that assumption. So, what if that assumption is wrong? What if no one is framing Minami? What would that mean then?"

Buddy cocked his head knowingly.

"Oh," Cora said.

The poodle was right.

Assuming no one was framing Minami, someone was framing her.

Cora had to find out why.

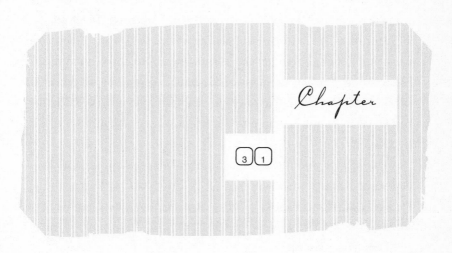

Chapter

3 1

Cora pulled the car to a stop half a block from Thelma Wilson's house. She had just killed the motor when the front door opened and Dennis Pride came out. He looked more businesslike than usual, and it wasn't just the three-piece suit, his briefcase, and the fact that his long hair was slicked back. No, for once Sherry's ne'er-do-well ex-husband had a purposeful stride and a serious air. Cora was sure the young man would slip into his usual flippant, obnoxious self if he were aware he was being observed, but for the moment he was one somber son of a bitch.

Cora wondered how his interview with Mrs. Wilson had gone.

Dennis crossed the street, climbed into his rental car, and drove off.

Cora ducked down behind the steering wheel as he went by, but Dennis was too preoccupied to even notice her car. She waited until he disappeared in the distance, then got out and walked up to the house.

Mrs. Wilson was a little older than Cora had figured. Of course, everyone looked young to her these days. An upward revision was the norm. In Mrs. Wilson's case it was warranted. The woman's face was lined and looked paler in artificial light. She ushered Cora into a living room furnished with way more doilies than the usual ration. She sat her guest on a spindly couch and sat opposite in a wicker chair that was either antique or just old. Cora suspected that in other circumstances the woman might have offered tea.

"You're here about the murder," Mrs. Wilson said, then nodded in agreement with herself. "Of course you are. You're the Puzzle Lady. Always looking into crime. As if it was a puzzle. I suppose it is. So, what does Chief Harper say?"

"I beg your pardon?"

"You're working with the police, aren't you?"

Cora was caught short by the woman's directness and had to take a moment to readjust her parameters. She smiled, said, "I'm not a police officer."

"Of course not. But you work with the police. Maybe not officially. But you do."

"Yes."

"So what's going on? I'd love to know. The woman was my neighbor. Not exactly a friend, perhaps, but an acquaintance. And then for such a terrible thing to happen. Do the police have any idea who did it?"

"Not at the present time."

"But they have that woman in jail. That doesn't mean she's guilty. I would find that hard to believe. I'm sure you do, too. There must be some other explanation."

"Can you think of one?"

"I beg your pardon?"

"That's the thing," Cora said. "Someone killed her. Whoever it was had to be in the house. And you didn't see anyone else go in or out."

She frowned. "That's a funny way to put it."

"What do you mean?"

"To tell me I didn't see anyone else go in or out. Wouldn't the normal thing be to *ask* me if I saw anyone go in or out?"

"Absolutely," Cora said. "And I'm assuming if you *had* seen someone, you would have mentioned it. That's why I said you didn't. Feel free to contradict me."

She considered that. "Hmm."

Cora took the opportunity to change the subject. "As I drove up, I noticed a young man leaving."

"Is that right? A young man, you say?"

"Yes. Coming out of your house."

"That's very interesting."

"Why is it interesting?"

"If I understand it correctly, the young man in question used to be married to your niece. I'm surprised you wouldn't know him."

"I *do* know him."

"And yet you call him a young man, as if you had no idea who he was."

"*I* know who he is. I didn't know if *you* knew."

"And if I didn't, you weren't going to help me?"

Cora took a breath. Good lord, what was she doing, pulling her punches just because she was afraid the woman might have seen her? "The young man. Dennis Pride. My niece's ex-husband. Do you know him?"

She smiled. "I do now."

"You hadn't met him before?"

"No."

"Why did he come to call?"

"You have to ask? The murder, of course."

"What's his interest in the affair?"

Her eyes twinkled. "What's yours?"

Cora felt a slight chill. "As you pointed out, I consult with Chief Harper. Dennis Pride doesn't."

She nodded. "You do seem to have a monopoly on the chief's time."

"So what did Dennis Pride want to know?"

"Is it relevant?"

"Yes, it is. I'm investigating the crime. Anyone who's interested interests me."

She nodded her head. "That's a reasonable explanation."

"I'm glad you approve. Do you think you could satisfy my curiosity?"

"I should think it was obvious. He wanted to know what I saw."

"What did you tell him?"

"The same thing I told the chief."

"And what was that?"

"You were there when I told him."

"I was there when you came out of your house. I thought you might have had a more extensive conversation later."

"The facts remain the same. I saw the Japanese woman twice. Once alone, once with her niece."

"You didn't see anyone else?"

"Again with the assumption."

"Sorry. *Did* you see anyone else?"

"That's exactly what Mr. Pride wanted to know."

Cora took a breath. "And what did you tell him?"

"The truth, of course."

Cora wanted to wring the woman's neck. "And what might that be?"

She studied Cora's face. "You're very clever. Just like the other woman. Do you like her much?"

"I beg your pardon?"

"Because I wouldn't think you would. You're rivals and all that. In the same field. Most women don't care for that at all. Were you glad they found the sudoku? That was a bit of luck. A clue pointing at your rival."

"I fail to see how it points at her."

"She's in jail."

"Because you saw her go in the house."

"So? If I'd seen you go in the house, you'd be in jail."

"What's that supposed to mean?"

"Just what it says. She's in jail, not because I saw her go in the house but because she went into the house. She did it. It was her action. It had nothing to do with me. You make it sound as if it's my fault she's in jail."

"I wasn't fixing blame."

"If I'd seen you go in the house, I bet you would. Suppose I told the police that? Would you be so understanding then?"

"If you lied to the police?"

"Lied? Who said anything about lying? We're playing a game of what-if. What if I came forward and said I saw you going into the house?"

"I would be most unhappy."

"I bet you would."

Cora pursed her lips. "You try this line on Dennis Pride?"

"What line?"

"Don't be coy. You're either very smart or totally oblivious. I'm trying to figure out which."

Mrs. Wilson smiled. "When you do, will you let me know?"

Thelma Wilson felt very pleased with herself. She'd played the game perfectly, set things up beautifully. Now there remained but to reap her reward. The reward she so richly deserved. It was galling to watch people out the window, coming and going and to-ing and fro-ing in their oh-so-important manner in their oh-so-important lives. It was nice when they got a little comeuppance now and then.

It was doubly nice that she was the one who knew it.

There was only one problem. Too many suspects. Too many possibilities for excitement. How to choose?

Of course, the police had first choice. That was a given. They picked the crazy Japanese lady. Which was good. Mrs. Wilson wouldn't have picked her. She wasn't comfortable dealing with foreigners. She never knew what they were thinking. Whether they were hiding something or being tripped up by a language barrier, confused by English idiom and confusing her in the process. No, the Sudoku Lady was out. Or, if not out, at least dropped to the bottom of the list.

The young one was a little different. More assimilated. More American. Mrs. Wilson could deal with her. As well as she could deal with any teenager. Which wasn't very. Youngsters were another country unto themselves, with their iPods and their downloads and their text messages and their MP3s, and what-have-you. Not that she'd had any personal contact with teenagers, mind you, but the ones she'd seen on TV were enough to put the girl near the bottom of the list, just ahead of her aunt.

That did not leave her with a lack of choices. She had more than enough to keep her happy. She just didn't know which to pick. She'd have to rattle their cages. See who stirred. How best to do that?

The kettle whistled. Mrs. Wilson went into the kitchen, brewed some tea. Tea always sharpened her focus, made her think. She couldn't imagine why more people didn't drink tea. A rejection of Old World values, no doubt. The Boston Tea Party and all that.

Mrs. Wilson let the tea steep, contemplated a cookie, planned her first move. It was a process of elimination. She needed to get people out of the way. How would that work? It depended on the person. For some, the direct approach. For others, bait.

What kind of bait? Well, that depended on the type of people she was attempting to lure. The Puzzle Lady was easy. Too easy. But the others. How to interest them?

Mrs. Wilson picked up her cup and saucer, carried her tea into the study, and sat at the writing desk. It was an old wooden rolltop with cubbyholes she'd gotten at a yard sale, not an antique shop—they ripped you off, always charging too much for anything worth having. Garage sales, attic sales, tag sales, that was where the bargains lay.

All right, the Japanese lady. She was in jail, but they couldn't keep her forever. When they released her, where would she be? Motel or bed-and-breakfast? Motel was more likely. She was a foreigner; she wouldn't be familiar with local customs. She might not understand bed-and-breakfast. Motels were easy. You saw a sign; you got a room. No thinking involved. Of course, she was a woman prone to thinking. Who solved puzzles. But not word puzzles. Number puzzles. Would that make a difference? These experts could be very good at their given field but socially gauche. Could they ever! Like that twerp of an accountant she'd never married. No, not nearly.

Her mind going a mile a minute, Thelma Wilson pulled out the phone book, looked up MOTELS. She checked the number and dialed.

"Hello? I'd like to leave a message for the Sudoku Lady . . . you know, the Japanese woman. I'm not sure what unit she's in. Could you leave a message for her? . . . She's not? I'm sorry, I must be misinformed."

Mrs. Wilson broke the connection, then dialed the next motel.

It took three. The manager of the Nutmeg Motel out on Kingston Road knew exactly who she was talking about and was happy to leave a message.

Mrs. Wilson gave him a phony number. "Could you ask her to call Mrs. Witness. First initial I. Thank you."

There. That ought to shake Minami up, being asked to call Mrs. I. Witness.

So, that took care of the Sudoku Lady. Now for the Puzzle Lady.

Mrs. Wilson took out a pen and paper and began writing.

Cora was not surprised to see Mrs. Cushman smiling. Mrs. Cushman was always smiling. The owner of Cushman's Bake Shop was a plump, doughy-faced woman who gave the impression she spent the whole day baking. Nothing could have been further from the truth. In point of fact, the woman couldn't bake a lick. Her muffins and scones were trucked in daily from the Silver Moon Bakery, and her genial smile actually reflected the serenity of being secure in the knowledge her wares came from the best bakery in New York.

"You have a note."

Cora frowned. She thought she was familiar with all of Mrs. Cushman's greetings, but that was a new one. "A note?"

"Yes. On the bulletin board."

The bulletin board on the wall of Cushman's Bake Shop served two purposes. It gave people something to peruse while waiting on line, and it allowed people to advertise such services as math tutoring, piano lessons, and tag sales. Some of the regulars would leave messages for one another. Cora had never done it, but she had seen the slips of paper thumbtacked to the board.

"Who left it?"

"Didn't notice. It's in the top-right corner." Mrs. Cushman pointed in that general direction and went to make a latte.

Cora's note was a piece of paper folded in fourths, which made it one of the larger messages on the board. Most weren't much more than a Post-it. Her name, Cora Felton, was printed on it in black fountain pen. Cora pulled out the pushpin, unfolded the note.

It was a crossword puzzle.

The Puzzle Lady vs. The Sudoku Lady

ACROSS

1 Turn on an axis
5 Element #30
9 "Great!"
14 Many a beer
15 "On the Waterfront" director Kazan
16 Balderdash
17 Invitation part 1
19 Take down a peg
20 Six in a million?
21 Kind of moss
23 Refusals
24 Remove, as marks
25 Invitation part 2
27 Confront
29 Stick in one's ___
30 With 41 Across, amount to bring
34 Glaswegian gal
36 Band together
39 Think tank member
41 See 30 Across
43 Lone Ranger's sidekick

A young woman in line holding a baby peered over Cora's shoulder. "Oh, look, someone left you a crossword puzzle. Are you going to solve it?"

"I'm most certainly not," Cora said grimly.

Cora went out, got in her car, and drove home.

Sherry wasn't there. Which meant Aaron must have dropped her someplace. It occurred to Cora *they* should have a bulletin board with pushpins to leave notes for one another, with so many people in the house. Of course, she was getting *out* of the house. In theory.

All right, how do you solve a crossword puzzle when you can't solve a crossword puzzle?

You bite the bullet.

Cora got back in the car, drove to Harvey Beerbaum's house. While Sherry and Aaron were on their honeymoon, Harvey had copped to the fact that Cora couldn't solve puzzles, a deduction on his part not nearly as miraculous as the number of years it had taken him to make it. And he was only half right. Harvey believed Cora could construct crossword puzzles; she just couldn't solve them. But in point of fact, she couldn't do either. However, for Harvey, half right was a triumph. Except when it came to puzzles, the man was remarkably dense.

Harvey came to the front door in a dinner jacket and a cummerbund.

"My, my," Cora said, "I didn't ask you to dress."

Harvey frowned. "You didn't tell me you were coming."

"No, I didn't. Under the circumstances, this is quite an honor. Do you always parade around in a monkey suit?"

"I'm giving an award. At a charity crossword puzzle convention. You really should go."

"Oh, I would," Cora said, "except I'm . . ." She waved her hand. "Oh, fill in the blank. I'm too stressed to come up with an excuse. The point is, I got another crossword puzzle dumped in my lap and I need you to solve it."

"I thought Sherry solved your puzzles."

"She does when she's home. She's out somewhere."

"It's that urgent?"

"I won't know until you tell me what it says."

"Does this have anything to do with the murders?"

"I don't know."

"Was it found at a crime scene?"

"It was on the bulletin board at Cushman's Bake Shop."

Harvey's face fell. "Oh."

"I'm sorry it's not dripping blood, Harvey. Can you solve it for me?"

"Oh. Yes, of course."

"Wanna invite me in, Harvey? You look like the doorman at the Hungarian consulate."

Harvey's living room was furnished in the style of IKEA and Louis Quatorze. A sprinkling of crossword puzzle memorabilia completed the decor. Cora sat on the couch, watched Harvey whiz through the puzzle. He did it so quickly she wondered if he actually retained a word.

"What's the theme entry?" Cora asked.

Harvey confirmed her theory by looking back at the paper.

"It's 'At three P.M., I'll be home. Bring cash. Come alone.'" He looked up quizzically. "What does that mean?"

Cora shrugged. "I don't know."

"And look at 30 Across: 'With 41 Across, amount to bring.' The answer to 30 Across is 'five,' and the answer to 41 Across is 'hundred.' So the amount to bring is five hundred. That must mean dollars. Someone wants someone to bring five hundred dollars to their home at three P.M.? Is that what it means?"

"I don't know," Cora said.

But she did.

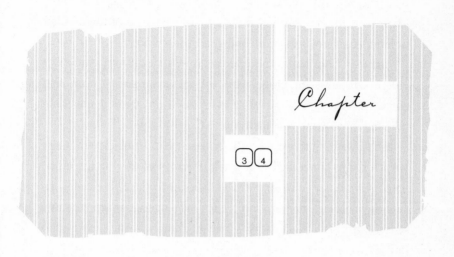

Chapter

3 4

Cora hated spying on people. Well, actually she liked it. But only when it was of her own volition. She didn't like to be coerced into it. Enticed into it. By some manipulative schemer. She had half a mind not to go.

Yeah, right. The woman goes to all the trouble to create a crossword puzzle in order to lure her into an intricate trap, she at least ought to find out what her game was.

She wasn't concerned with who. That was easy. Thelma Wilson stuck out like a sore thumb. She was the witness, the enigmatic woman of a thousand twitches. If Cora were the chief of police, she'd have locked her up. Unfortunately, Cora wasn't the chief of police. Dale Harper was the chief of police, and he would require more than her say-so to make an arrest. Cora had nothing to go on, just a stinking crossword puzzle. Still, she should have brought him with her. Only he wouldn't have come. And if he had, he'd have queered her game. Could you still use that expression, or was it politically incorrect? Cora had had it with the PC police. As far as she was concerned, freedom of speech ought to allow her to say any damn thing she wanted, regardless of the number of letters in the words or meaning in the subtext.

Anyway, Cora had to find out what was afoot. And she wasn't worried about going alone. After all, she was packing heat. And as far as Thelma Wilson was concerned, Cora figured she could take her. That's why she hadn't told Chief Harper.

It had nothing to do with the undercurrent of blackmail. Cora wasn't really concerned that Thelma had seen her at the crime scene. Or that anyone might have seen her at the crime scene, assuming the blackmailer wasn't Thelma. Not that that made any sense. If the blackmailer wasn't Thelma, how was she supposed to know?

What if it was Minami? Wouldn't that be a kick. Only she was in jail. For the same transgression for which she'd be blackmailing Cora. That was convoluted even for her.

Cora parked a block and a half away, sat in the car. Weighed her options. There weren't many. She could either go or not. Not going wasn't an option. That left going. Cora hated that. It was like being forced to go.

Cora did *not* have five hundred dollars with her. She had rebelled at that. Bring cash, indeed. No way. If she was being blackmailed, she would confront her blackmailer and say, Do your worst. Publish and be damned. Or, tell Chief Harper and be damned. Actually, tell Chief Harper and *she'd* be damned.

What a mess. It was almost worth five hundred dollars to get out of it. Not that she'd pay it in a million years. Just in practical terms.

Cora waited for the minutes to tick down to three P.M.

To hell with that! If the woman was home, she could see her at Cora's convenience.

Cora got out of the car and started for the house. It was twenty to three. Early enough to seem intentionally early. Cora liked that. She went up the steps and rang the bell.

Waited.

There was no answer.

Cora rang again. Nothing. She jabbed the button repeatedly. She could hear the bell ringing inside the house. No one was home. Either that or the woman was making her wait, playing a mind game of her own.

Cora tried the doorknob.

It clicked open.

Uh oh.

She pushed the door open, stepped inside.

"Mrs. Wilson?"

There was no answer.

Cora closed the door behind her, tiptoed through the foyer into the living room.

Thelma Wilson lay facedown in front of the hearth. Her head had been bashed in. A poker lay on the floor beside her.

Cora graced the corpse with a brief eulogy, not particularly kind.

It occurred to her that at least this ought to get Minami off the hook. As long as the murders were connected. Though, how could they not be? The witness to one murder is rubbed out. It's gotta be the killer that did it. Too bad there wasn't a sudoku next to the corpse. That would ice it.

Cora looked around, but there was none. Too much to hope for.

Well, time to call the police. But not from this phone. She couldn't touch that. And she didn't have a cell phone. But she still had Sherry's. She'd borrowed it; had she given it back?

Cora jammed her hand down in her drawstring purse and fumbled around.

No phone. Just some papers. Cora pulled them out.

It was sudoku puzzles she'd been doing on the computer. One was finished, all ready to go. She looked it over. In every way it resembled the one found by the body of Sheila Preston. Different numbers, of course, but aside from that . . .

		9			8		2	
6		3	2				8	
	7		9	1			3	
	8	2		5			7	
				7			6	
		4		8				
								5
						3	4	
9		5		3		6		

Cora slapped the sudoku on the floor next to Thelma Wilson's body. She stood up, took a quick look around. Had she touched anything? No. Just the doorknob. No matter, she'd been there before.

Cora went out, closing the door behind her.

She drove straight to the mall, screeched to a stop, vaulted from the car, and hurried in the door, trying not to look conspicuous but moving as fast as she could.

There was a payphone on the wall just inside the entrance, a dinosaur left over from the time before there were cell phones. Cora prayed it was still there.

It was. Cora snatched up the receiver, got a dial tone.

Excellent.

She dug in her purse, pulled out a sudoku. Wadded it up, stuck it in her mouth. Chewed it around. Wasn't satisfied. She wadded up another, stuck it in her other cheek.

"Well," she said, "can you hear me now?"

That was debatable. She sounded like a cross between Marlon Brando in *The Godfather* and a drowning mule.

Cora dialed the police station.

Dan Finley answered the phone. "Bakerhaven Police."

"Rraargh!" Cora said.

"Excuse me?"

"Help!" she croaked.

"Did you say help?"

"Rraargh!"

"I can't understand you. What do you want?"

"Helmargh Vilsson!"

"Huh!"

"Helmargh Vilsson!"

"Thelma Wilson?"

"Arrrgh!!!"

Cora slammed down the phone, spat out the sudoku mush in

the trash. She got in her car and drove home. She figured that was her best shot. Dan got the name. She was sure of that. With any luck, he would figure someone was strangling Thelma Wilson, who had gotten away long enough to dial the phone. Of course, that wouldn't fly if they started checking phone records, but that wasn't the point.

Cora might have reported the killing, if not for the sudoku. Her being on the scene and the sudoku being found made it too big a coincidence. People would wonder if she was involved. She didn't want anyone getting the right idea.

There was a car in the driveway. A black sedan.

Dennis.

Son of a bitch!

Sneaking around when she wasn't there, surprising Sherry at home. Was she all right? Dennis wasn't stable where Sherry was concerned, could easily lose it. He could hurt her, whether he meant to or not.

Cora fumbled in her purse, gripped the butt of her gun, hurried up the path.

She reached the front door, flung it wide.

Minami and Michiko were sitting on the couch with Sherry. They looked up in surprise as the door banged open.

Cora gawked in amazement. "What are you doing here?"

"Cora, don't be rude. We have guests."

"See?" Michiko said. "We should have called."

"I did not know the number."

"That is no excuse."

Cora blinked. "You're here."

"Yes," Sherry said. "She's here. The police just let her go and she came to see you. We were having tea. Would you like some?"

Buddy, who'd been begging treats, circled Cora's feet and

darted outside. She called him back in, shut the door, stumbled over, and collapsed in a chair.

"There you go. Let me pour you some tea." Sherry picked up the pot, filled a cup, handed her the cup and saucer.

Cora took a sip to calm her nerves. "How did you get out of jail?" She asked Minami.

The Sudoku Lady smiled. "They had no evidence. They had to let me go."

"Isn't that wonderful?" Sherry said.

"Fantastic."

"So," Minami said, "the race is back on. We will see who can solve these murders first. There was not much that I could do in jail. You have a head start. It does not matter."

Cora sighed. "Oh, for goodness' sake."

Sherry frowned. "Cora, what's the matter?"

There came the sound of cars in the driveway.

"Excuse me. Someone else is here." Sherry got up and looked out the window.

Chief Harper and Dan Finley were striding up the path.

"It's the police. I wonder what they want."

"I have no idea," Cora said.

Sherry opened the door for the officers.

"Good afternoon, ladies," Chief Harper said. "Sorry to intrude, but we have a small problem." He jerked his thumb at Minami. "No sooner do I let her out of jail but a body shows up with a sudoku attached. I don't suppose you happen to know anything about that."

Minami's mouth fell open. "What?"

"Thelma Wilson's been murdered. In case you don't recognize the name—that's the woman who got you arrested for murder."

Harper shook his head.

"Looks like she's done it again."

"Sherry, I'm going mad."

"You expect me to argue with you?"

"Don't be cute. I'm getting old. Incompetent. Worst of all, my luck's run out. Everything I do is a disaster."

"Oh, come on."

"You know how many times in the past I've played fast and loose with the evidence? Of course you don't. When you get away with it, you don't have to tell. It's only the disasters that come back to haunt you."

Sherry looked up from the stove. "Cora, I am making pork tenderloin. It's tricky. You gotta be very careful not to overcook it."

It smelled delicious. The fact that Cora wasn't immediately distracted was a good indication of the extent of her emotional distress.

"I'm losing it, Sherry. I really am."

Sherry looked up in concern. Cora's comment about always getting away with it wasn't entirely accurate. She had taken some hard knocks, including getting arrested for murder. "Cora, what's wrong?"

"I framed Minami."

"What!?"

"I didn't mean to do it, but I did."

"What are you talking about?"

"I found Thelma Wilson dead."

"*You* found her?"

"Yeah."

"The police got an anonymous tip."

"That was me."

"And they didn't recognize your voice?"

"I was chewing sudoku."

"Chewing what?"

"Sudoku. Among other things. It doesn't matter. The point is I found her dead."

"Why were you even there?"

"She sent me a blackmail note."

"She was blackmailing you?"

"Yes."

"For what?"

"For finding the other body."

"Cora."

"I wasn't going to pay it, of course."

"Pay what?"

"The five hundred dollars."

"She demanded five hundred dollars?"

"That's right."

"She sent you a blackmail note? Was it cut from pieces of the newspaper?"

"Actually, it was a crossword puzzle."

"A crossword puzzle? You solved a crossword puzzle?"

"Harvey Beerbaum did. It told me to bring the money to her house at three o'clock. I wasn't going to, but I wanted to find out what her game was."

"So you went there and found the body."

"That's right."

"With a sudoku."

Cora grimaced. "That's the bad part."

Sherry's eyes widened. "Oh, my God!"

"Well, I thought it would be a swell break for Minami. The only thing that really connected her the first time was the sudoku. I thought wouldn't it be neat if a body turned up with a sudoku while she was in jail. They'd have to let her go."

"They *let* her go."

"I didn't know that."

"What a mess."

Cora shook her head. "I framed her for the crime; now I gotta clear her."

"How you gonna do that? Fess up?"

"Please."

"So, you're gonna work with Becky Baldwin?"

"Yes and no."

"What does that mean?"

"Well, on the one hand, she's hired me."

"That would seem like a yes."

"On the other hand, I framed her client."

"That sounds less positive."

"Yes. Of course, she doesn't know it yet."

"You haven't told her?"

"It's the sort of thing you hate to blurt out. That's one stumbling block. She also won't let me talk to her client."

"Why not?"

"I don't know. She's claiming attorney-client privilege. But why'd she have to do that with me?"

"When she doesn't know you framed her."

"Exactly. As far as she knows, I'm a perfectly loyal investigator, currently in her employ. Talking to her client would be the right and proper thing to do. But she doesn't want me to." Cora frowned. "There's a clue in there somewhere, if I knew what it was."

"Now you're seeing conspiracies everywhere."

"It's the flaw of conspiring. Which is why I tend to keep things to myself. Sorry to burden you with it, but I'm going a little nuts."

"Maybe you should see a therapist."

"Anyone who goes to a psychiatrist should have his head examined." Cora waggled an imaginary cigar. "Say the secret word, the duck will fly down and give you a hundred dollars. It's a common word, something you'll find around the house."

"Boy, you really are losing it. Why don't you go talk to Chief Harper?"

"I don't think he wants to talk to me."

"Why not?"

"For one thing, I'm working for the other side."

"That's never stopped him before. He doesn't know you planted evidence at the crime scene, does he?"

"Bite your tongue."

"So he's going to want you to solve it. Unless Minami did."

"The suspect? I doubt if he'd trust her. Even if he did, Becky wouldn't let her."

"There you are. It's the perfect icebreaker. Just solve the su-doku for him."

Cora grimaced. "Small problem."

"What?"

"If I do, he's gonna want to know what it means."

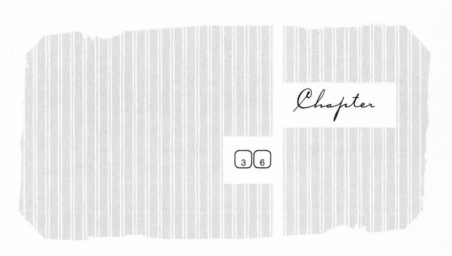

"You have to solve the puzzle."

"Oh, for God's sake!"

"What do you mean, for God's sake? You're a whiz at sudoku. It'll take you two minutes."

"So what?"

"So what? Then you can tell me what it means."

Cora grimaced. "See, Chief, I can't win. You throw a meaningless sudoku in my lap. If I don't solve it, you're pissed. If I do solve it, you want to know what it means."

"Well, it's not an academic interest," Harper said sarcastically. "I happen to have three murder cases."

"The sudoku won't help."

"Why not?"

"It's got nothing to do with anything."

"It was found at the scene of the crime."

"Oh, come on, Chief. That's a ridiculous idea. Why would Minami leave a sudoku next to the body? Now someone *else* might leave it to *frame* her, but why would *she* leave it? To frame *herself*?"

"I don't know *why* she did it, but it certainly looks like she did. After all, she creates sudoku puzzles."

"So do *I*. That doesn't mean *I* killed her."

"You had no motive. In Minami's case, she was the eyewitness, the woman who identified her, who sent her to jail."

"Wow," Cora said sarcastically, "with all that, she'd barely *need* to leave a sudoku to draw attention her way."

"Why are you defending her so vehemently? I thought you didn't like her."

"I don't. That doesn't mean I want to stick her with a gratuitous murder rap."

"If she didn't kill the woman, who did?"

"Whoever killed Sheila Preston."

"Which looks like her, too."

"How do you figure?"

"Minami's trying to solve the murder of Ida Fielding. She get's a line on Sheila Preston, starts poking around, finds out Sheila was aware of her husband's relationship with Ida. Sheila had every reason to want to kill Ida. Say she did. Say Minami suspects. She goads Sheila, hoping to get a nibble. Sheila realizes Minami's onto her, panics, tries to get her out of the way. Minami strikes first."

"You're claiming she killed her in self-defense?"

"That's up to the court to decide. I'm just gathering facts."

"You're gathering wild conjectures based on no evidence whatsoever."

Harper frowned. "Can you gather conjectures?"

"Don't play word games with me. I'm not in the mood."

Harper held up the sudoku. "How about number games?"

"Chief, forget the numbers. Concentrate on the crime. This woman was killed in her own house. Someone must have seen something. What do the neighbors say?"

"The neighbor across the street is dead."

"That is a problem."

"One next-door neighbor is ninety-two and deaf as a post. The other works in Danbury and was gone all day."

"Fine. No witnesses. We'll have to figure it out another way."

"Which brings us back to the sudoku."

Cora took a breath. "Chief, come on, think it through. The chief witness against Minami got murdered. After Minami got released from jail, granted. But if you look at it one way, that's a point in her favor. She's already identified her. Thelma Wilson did her worst, and it didn't stick. Minami's got nothing to fear from her. On the other hand, if the killer is someone *else*, someone Thelma *hasn't* identified, that's the person who has to fear. And with Minami out of jail, it means the police no longer suspect Minami and will concentrate on the real killer. Did Thelma Wilson see the real killer? The real killer can't be sure. What if Thelma Wilson identifies the real killer next? There's only one way to make sure that doesn't happen. What does the real killer do? Kills Thelma Wilson and leaves a sudoku."

"How would this real killer know Minami was out of jail?"

"How the hell should I know? Maybe the real killer's Dan Finley."

"Cora."

"I know he's not. But the real killer could be someone Dan Finley knows and told."

"Rick Reed?"

Cora cocked her head at the chief. "Now you're just screwing with me."

"Hey, if you can name Dan, I can name Rick." Harper picked up the sudoku from his desk. "You gonna solve it for me or not?"

"Fine, I'll solve it for you."

Cora whizzed through the puzzle.

1	4	9	3	6	8	5	2	7
6	5	3	2	4	7	9	8	1
2	7	8	9	1	5	4	3	6
3	8	2	6	5	9	1	7	4
5	9	1	4	7	2	8	6	3
7	6	4	1	8	3	2	5	9
4	3	6	8	2	1	7	9	5
8	1	7	5	9	6	3	4	2
9	2	5	7	3	4	6	1	8

Chief Harper took it, held it up. "So, what does it mean?"

"How the hell should I know?"

"You usually have a theory."

"I usually have something to go on. This time I don't. I have eighty-one numbers with no clue as to what their order means. You want to give me a hint as to how I should get going on a theory?"

"I have no idea."

"Me, neither."

"Okay, maybe you're right," Harper conceded. "Maybe the

numbers *don't* mean anything. Maybe the importance of the sudoku is just that it's a sudoku. The woman signed her crime. Thinking no one would believe it was actually her. Plus, the sudoku gives her a reason to investigate the crime as soon as she's cleared. Which she expects to be."

"That's really stupid."

"I wish you'd stop saying that. I'm going to get a complex."

"Chief, killers don't go around signing their crimes."

"I don't know. Wasn't there some strangler who left a white kid glove on all his victims?"

"That's different."

"Why?"

"He left his glove. Not his American Express card."

"Isn't a sudoku more like a glove?"

"Probably not as warm. Chief, forget the sudoku. It doesn't point to Minami. It points away from Minami. It screams to high heaven that Minami had nothing to do with it."

"And you know that because . . . ?"

"Because I can think and reason."

"Uh huh," Harper said. If he was convinced, Cora wouldn't have known it. He picked up a paper from his desk. "We have one other lead."

"Oh?"

"And I think this one might help. The phone call Dan Finley got."

"What about it?"

"It was presumably Thelma Wilson being strangled. But it wasn't."

"Oh?"

Chief Harper shook his head. "Didn't come from her phone. We traced the records and it came from the mall."

Cora frowned. "That makes no sense."

"Tell me about it. Unless you'd like to argue that Thelma Wilson was strangled in the mall and the body brought back to her house. I don't think you want to argue that."

"Particularly since she *wasn't* strangled."

"Exactly. Then the call was from someone who wanted to tip us off to the crime. Most likely from the murderer himself."

Cora took a breath. "How do you figure?"

"At that point in time, only the murderer himself knew she was dead. According to the medical examiner, she was just killed. If the murderer hopped in his car and drove to the mall, he could make that call and tip the cops off so the body would be found. For some reason, it was to the murderer's advantage to have the body found right away. Either because of an alibi the murderer had established. Or perhaps because of an alibi someone the murderer was framing *didn't* have. It could be lots of reasons."

"You're saying murderer."

"So?"

"Dan Finley thought the caller was Thelma Wilson. He thought it was a woman."

"He thought it was a person being strangled. Or someone approximating a person being strangled. He couldn't swear to the gender. It's a wonder he even got the name. But you're right, the caller was most likely a woman. So. If Minami gets out of jail, goes straight to Thelma Wilson's, kills her, drives to the mall, makes that phone call, what time would she arrive at your house?"

"That's absurd."

"Oh? Why is it absurd? According to Barney Nathan, it's highly unlikely Thelma Wilson was alive when the call was made. It's legal doubt, a lawyer might argue, but not the type of thing

I have to get hung up on. As far as I'm concerned, it was probably from the killer."

"Why would the killer want to tip you off?"

"So the body would be found."

"Why would the killer care?"

"So we'd pinpoint the time of the murder and know it happened right after Minami got out of jail."

"Then Minami isn't the killer."

Harper frowned.

"Unless you figure Minami made the call, in which case, explain to me why she would do that."

"I have no idea why she'd do that."

"Then your whole theory falls apart. That call proves, by irrefutable logic, that Minami couldn't have done it."

"It proves nothing of the sort."

Cora waggled her hand. "Mmm. Wait'll you hear Becky Baldwin tell it."

"Spare me."

"No, if the whole case hinges on the theory Minami made that call, you're screwed, blued, and tattooed." Cora frowned. "I'm not entirely sure what that means, but it sounds good, doesn't it? No way in hell she makes that call. For no reason whatsoever. The call can only be the work of someone who knows Minami's been let out of jail and wants to let her take the blame."

"So you say. But there could be a million reasons for calling. It could simply be some innocent bystander who doesn't want to come forward. We get that type of call all the time."

"You can't have an innocent bystander to a murder. If he's a bystander, he isn't innocent. He's an accessory, at best."

"It's possible Minami had an accomplice."

Cora groaned. "There you go, off on the wrong tangent, just

like a donkey after a carrot. If Minami had an accomplice, the accomplice would have the same motivations as Minami. The accomplice wouldn't be doing things to *implicate* Minami. The accomplice would be doing things to *exonerate* Minami. Good lord, why do I even bother?"

Chief Harper looked at her narrowly. "You're certainly vehement about this."

"Well, it's so obvious."

"Things have been obvious before. And I have stated opposing views, just playing devil's advocate. It usually spurs your creative mind. This time it infuriates you. I wonder why that is."

"If you're going to do a psychological profile on me, I'm leaving."

"That reaction is interesting, too."

"No, no, no! You can't have it both ways. You can't be annoying, and say, 'Aha! I'm annoying you, that must mean something!'"

"Maybe not, but it's certainly fun." He smiled. "I haven't had fun in a long time. You should try it, Cora. Competition makes you cranky."

"You think this is cranky. You ain't seen nothin' yet."

Cora left the police station in a foul mood. Chief Harper had only two leads: the sudoku and the phone call.

And she was responsible for both of them.

Harvey Beerbaum looked distraught. "Cora! Tell me you didn't
do it!"

"I didn't do it."

"But—"

"Gonna ask me in, Harvey?"

"Sorry. Come in." Harvey stepped aside and ushered her into
his living room. "I'm forgetting my manners. Would you like
some tea?"

"Are you going to call the police while you make it?"

"Of course not. Why do you say that?"

"You're scrupulous to a fault. You probably figure it's your
duty."

"But . . ."

"But what?"

"There's no evidence."

"That's the spirit."

"But I have information."

"What information?"

"The crossword puzzle."

"What about it?"

"*'At three P.M., I'll be home. Bring cash; come alone.'* That's when Thelma Wilson was killed."

"How do you know when she was killed?"

"Well, approximately."

"Close only counts in horseshoes, Harvey. The police don't know when she was killed. I don't think Barney Nathan's even given an estimate yet."

"Even so."

"There's no reason to assume the crossword puzzle had anything to do with her. If you insist on going to the police, it will prove nothing. Except that you can't be trusted. And I can never show you another crossword puzzle."

"Oh, I say!"

Cora put up her hand. "No, you *don't* say. That's the whole point. What you *don't* say. Harper has enough trouble trying to solve this crime without going off on a wild goose chase because you gave him a false lead based on a crossword puzzle."

Harvey looked closely at her. "Are you telling me you *didn't* go over there?"

"Are you cross-examining me, Harvey?"

"No. Just asking a question."

"What's the difference?"

"You're the wordsmith."

"Why, Harvey Beerbaum, that's the nicest thing you've ever said to me."

"What?"

Cora batted her eyes. "You're just saying that, aren't you?"

Harvey, flustered, stammered, "What?"

"Oh, you sly dog, Harvey. I didn't know you had it in you."

Harvey plowed through the blarney. "Wait a minute. You're saying you never went near Thelma Wilson's house?"

"Thelma Wilson's house? Who said anything about Thelma Wilson's house?"

"The crossword puzzle."

"What crossword puzzle? I don't recall any crossword puzzle found in Thelma Wilson's house."

"You know what I mean."

"No, Harvey, I only know what you *say*. As you so aptly pointed out, I am a wordsmith. Words have meaning. I have to listen to your words and hear what they say. You said the crossword puzzle had something to do with Thelma Wilson's house. It clearly doesn't. I defy you to point out one instance in the crossword puzzle where Thelma Wilson's house is mentioned."

"You're twisting words."

"Twisting words? First I'm a wordsmith, forging words with hammer and anvil; now I'm a contortionist, twisting words into a pretzel."

"Contortionists twist their bodies."

"You're getting personal again, Harvey. Let's get down to brass tacks. I don't want you to give the puzzle to Chief Harper. Are you going to do it?"

Harvey frowned. "No."

Cora smiled and spread her hands. "Then we have no problem."

"I've got big problems."

Becky Baldwin speared a cherry tomato out of her salad. "Do you really? I've got a client on the hook for two murders. Granted, I need the work. Still, in the current state of the economy, I'm not sure this is a good bet. How's the dollar doing against the yen?"

"Isn't that China?"

"Really? What's Japan?"

"A country."

"You're not helping. Or, right, the yen's Japanese. Don't you know that? I thought you got royalties."

"Sherry handles them."

Becky shook her head. "You're going to be lost when you move out."

"How can I help? You won't let me talk to your client. You won't let me talk to her niece. You won't even let me talk to you."

"You can talk to me."

"Why can't I talk to your client?"

"There are certain admissions she wishes to make only to her attorney."

"There you are. What's the good of talking to you if you won't tell me anything?"

"I'll tell you anything you need to know."

"I need to know what you're not telling me."

"Actually, you don't. You need to approach the problem from the point of view that you know everything. That nothing you don't know will hurt you. That you know everything pertinent to the crime."

"Now you're intriguing me. Are you telling me your client is holding back something not pertinent to the crime?"

Becky chewed a carrot. "I'm telling you nothing of the sort. I'm telling you you're getting hung up on irrelevant details when we have the broader picture to consider. The situation is simple. Someone killed Thelma Wilson, and it wasn't Minami. Who was it?"

Cora made a face. "Oh, for goodness' sake! You're like the algebra teacher who puts a problem up on the board, and when you ask a question about procedure, she says, 'That's not important, just solve it.'"

"You have trouble with algebra?"

"I have trouble with you. You're like a patient who goes to a doctor and says, 'I got a pain here. It's gallstones. They gotta come out.' Should the doctor take 'em out? Or do you think he should make his own examination?"

"You're big on analogies today."

"Because you won't talk about the situation."

"Yes, I will. I just won't talk about my client. Which is okay, since she had nothing to do with it."

"Who did?"

"I should think it was obvious. Thelma Wilson was a nosy old biddy who saw something and tried to put the bite on someone. In which case, she must have made the initial approach. So, how do you suppose she contacted her victim?"

"I have no idea."

Becky shook her head. "See? This is what bothers me. Usually you have plenty of ideas. Suddenly you're stymied. Why? Is it the rivalry? Subconsciously you don't want to help Minami?"

"That's not true. *Consciously* I don't want to help Minami. I'd like to see her fall in a mud puddle. I'd like to see her with egg on her face. Is that just an expression, or could I really throw eggs at her? I'd like to see her prove herself wrong. I do *not* want to see her convicted of a murder she didn't commit. I'm working toward that end. In spite of the roadblocks you keep throwing in my path."

"Then, help me out here. Say Thelma Wilson saw someone else go into that house. Who might that person be? Aside from you and Dennis Pride."

"I never said I went into the house."

"Right, right. I don't know where I got that impression. Anyway, who could it be?"

"Either of the husbands."

"Oh?"

"Sure. Either of them kills the first wife. Gets suspected by the second wife. Kills her. Gets seen by Thelma Wilson and kills her. What could be simpler?"

"I like it. Largely because it doesn't involve Minami. Still, I like it. It's so simple it almost has to be true." Becky nibbled a radish. "It's depressing to think it isn't."

"Why do you say that?"

"Because if the crime was that simple, Chief Harper would have solved it by now. I can't imagine either of these husbands would be that tough to break down. He grilled 'em without finding a crack. And you talked to both of them, haven't you?"

"Yeah."

"And so has Minami. And you've all come up empty." Becky cocked her head. "I can't help thinking there's someone else Thelma Wilson saw going into that house."

Michiko turned into the motel parking lot and stopped in front of the unit she shared with her aunt.

A car pulled up next to hers. Dennis Pride hopped out and leaned on the open door. He grinned. "You old enough to drive?"

"What are you doing here?"

"My civic duty. We can't have kids driving around the streets of Bakerhaven. I may have to make a citizen's arrest."

"I can drive."

"I see that. And well, too, I must say. That's not the question. The question is if you have a legal right."

"I have a license."

"An American license?"

"I don't need an American license."

"You're not licensed in the United States?"

"It's good."

"Let's see."

"I don't have to show you. You are not the police."

"No, but I could tell them."

"Why would you do that?"

"Well, if you're not going to show me your license."

"Fine. I'll show you my license."

Michiko dug in her purse, pulled out the license, and held it up.

Dennis squinted at it. "I can't read this. It's in Japanese."

"So?"

"How do I know it's a license? It could be a library card."

"You don't believe me?"

"Why should I?"

"What do you want?"

"I want to talk to you."

"Out here?"

"Well, I'm not going in there. I could get arrested just for being in the same room with you."

"I am not a child."

"No, you're not. You're a big girl whose aunt's in jail. Again. She keeps bumping women off. And you're supposed to be keeping her out of trouble. This is not going to look good on your résumé."

"That is not what I do."

"Oh? What do you do?"

"I am not a babysitter."

"I'm glad to hear it."

"Minami does not do the stupid things you say. She's smart, she solves crime, and she is very famous. And you don't know what you are talking about."

"So she didn't get a blackmail note?"

Michiko's eyes flicked.

Dennis grinned. "She did, didn't she? Have you told the police? You haven't, have you? I hope you destroyed the note."

Michiko pouted. "I am not talking to you anymore."

"Too bad. Now I have to tell the police to ask you about a blackmail note."

"You're not going to do that."

"Says who?"

"What?"

"You're not familiar with that expression? It's short for, 'Oh yeah, who says I'm not?' You get that one? It means I'll go to the police if I want to."

"Stay away from the police."

"Well, if you're not going to talk to me, I really have no choice."

Michiko said nothing.

"Are you going to talk to me?"

She set her jaw.

"Okay, I'll just go to the police."

"If you go to the police, I will never talk to you again. You will lose your power."

"Maybe it's worth it."

"It is not worth losing your power."

"It is if my power's not worth anything. Okay, I'll stay away from the police. But get a message to your aunt. Tell her she's not the only one who knows about the blackmail note. Tell her the only reason the police don't know is because I'm such a kind-hearted fellow. And ask her if she'd like to talk to me. I think she'd like to talk to me. Which should be easy. We have the same lawyer. And our lawyer's keeping us apart. If your aunt doesn't like it, she doesn't have to put up with it. I have a feeling she doesn't. She's not the type of woman who likes to remain silent. So see what she wants to do."

"I do not have to take your advice."

"She's in jail. Maybe you like that because it leaves you free to run around. But you don't know anybody. You can't be having much fun. So you're probably a pretty unhappy girl long about now. Go talk to your aunt and try to get her to listen to reason. You'll be doing her a favor."

Dennis hopped in his car and drove off.

Michiko watched him go.

She bit her lip and wondered what to do.

Chapter

4 0

Irving Swartzman was at his sartorial best in yellow shirt, green tie, and pinstripe suit. He was all Rick Reed had been able to corral, what with Becky and her client not talking, and the flashy agent was doing his damndest to seize the moment.

"An author, a *famous* author, comes here from Japan to meet her public. And what happens? She is *arrested*, not *once* but *twice*, on the charge of *murder*. On the flimsiest evidence whatsoever. And the only reason she has not demonstrated her innocence and gone free—as she clearly is—is because of an antiquated legal system that punishes the innocent for any given remark and forces their lawyers to advise them to remain silent.

"Minami, the Sudoku Lady, has absolutely nothing to hide. Yet she is a foreigner. English is her second language. If she were to misstate, misconstrue, or misunderstand some English idiom, some unscrupulous prosecutor could seize on such a statement and manipulate a credulous jury into believing that such an innocent error was an open indication of guilt.

"No, it is no wonder she is not talking. It *is* a wonder that the police are holding her. Anyone with half a brain could see what is happening here. The Sudoku Lady has a knack for solving crime. The killer, realizing she was his biggest threat, decided to frame her to get her off his back. Any idiot could see that. The Sudoku Lady did not come here to kill people."

Irving Swartzman popped open his briefcase. "She came here to promote her book: *Solving Sudoku with the Sudoku Lady.* Available in the United States in a new English translation. That is the reason she's here, and that's the only reason she's here. And if you need any corroboration of that fact, go to Amazon.com. And check it out."

Cora gaped at the television. "Son of a bitch!"

"Yeah," Aaron said, "pretty sleazy."

"Sleazy, hell! The woman didn't come to America to meet me. She came to promote a book! I'm her inroad to the American mainstream media. The Sudoku Lady meets the Puzzle Lady, swaps a few war stories, and whips out the English translation of her brand-spanking-new sudoku book. That didn't happen because we had a murder, and Minami decided she could get more mileage out of solving it, only she got arrested and can't say anything. Her agent finally got fed up with waiting. Which is actually a good move because her being in-jail-for-murder with a book out is better than her being a snoopy-old-woman-giving-the-police-a-hard-time with a book out."

"And you know from whence you speak," Sherry observed.

Cora wished activities upon her niece that are inappropriate for a newlywed.

Sherry didn't respond. She was busy typing on her laptop.

"What are you doing?"

"Got a wireless modem. I'm on the Internet."

"In here?" Cora said. As usual, they were dining in the living room in front of the TV.

"Sherry can get on the Internet anywhere," Aaron said.

"There," Sherry said, "Amazon.com. And there it is. *Solving Sudoku with the Sudoku Lady*. Available for preorder. The pub date's the first of the month. At the moment it's sales rank is forty-seven thousand, five hundred twenty-two. Your Puzzle Lady book is two thousand seventy-one."

"Two *thousand*?" Cora said.

"That's out of everything. Fiction, nonfiction, children's books, advice on how-to. In *Puzzle Books* you're fourteen."

"Fourteen?"

"That's in *all* puzzle books. Including crosswords and KenKen. In sudoku, you're number three, just behind two titles from Will Shortz. Minami's new book is fifty-eight."

"In sudoku? Are there that many books?"

"There are hundreds. Fifty-eight's pretty good for a book that isn't out yet."

"And she's forty-seven thousand over all?"

"Something like that. Let me check." Sherry punched in the title. "Actually, she's up to thirty-three thousand."

"Oh?"

"Which doesn't mean anything. When the numbers are that high, just a few books makes a huge difference. You, on the other hand, are hanging in around two thousand."

Buddy went nuts. He sprang off the couch and raced from the room, yipping wildly.

"Someone must be here," Aaron said.

"Or he didn't like my Amazon.com rating," Cora said.

Sherry went to the front door and ushered in Michiko.

The teenager wasted no time with amenities. "I have to talk to you."

"What's the problem?" Aaron said.

Her eyes flashed. "Not you. You work for the newspaper. I cannot talk to you."

"He's married to *her*," Cora said. "He doesn't work for the paper if she says he doesn't."

Michiko frowned. "What?"

"When you're older, you'll understand. Maybe 'understand' is the wrong word. But you'll know it's true. If she tells him not to write it, he won't write it."

"Wait a minute," Aaron said. "I'm getting third-hand off the record? She's telling you to tell her to tell me not to write it. Come on, have a heart."

"Don't be silly, Aaron. No one's telling you what to write. If you'd like to preserve your journalistic integrity, you're free to go."

"I *live* here."

"See?" Cora said. "There *is* a boundary dispute. I keep thinking of this as my house. Really, us all living here isn't going to work."

"For goodness' sake," Sherry said, "will you two stop bickering. Look, she's all upset."

Michiko clearly was distraught.

"Oh, hell, so she is. Look, Aaron, the girl can't deal with this. Are we off the record, or shall I take her somewhere else?"

"We're off the record, we're off the record! Look, Michiko, you have my word. Whatever you say, I won't write it. It will *not* be in my story. Go ahead, say whatever you want. You're not going to get into trouble."

"It's that horrible man."

"What horrible man?"

"The one she married. No, not you. The other one."

"Dennis?" Aaron said. "What's he done?"

"He threatened me."

Cora sprang from the couch, her eyes blazing. "He *threatened* you?"

Michiko put up her hands. "No. Not to hurt me. With the police."

"He said he would go to the police?"

"Yes."

"And tell them what?"

"Oh."

"You don't want to tell us?"

"No."

"I know. But you're going to. It'll be much easier if you just do it and get it over with. So, take your time. Take a deep breath. Relax. And tell us the thing you don't want to tell us."

Michiko scrunched up her face. Then she sighed. "He said he would tell them she got a blackmail note."

"How does he know that?"

"He doesn't. He is guessing."

"Is he guessing right?"

Michiko said nothing.

"It wouldn't bother you if he wasn't. So your aunt got a blackmail note. Interesting. What did it say?"

"I have it here."

Michiko reached into her purse. Took out a folded piece of paper. Passed it over.

Cora unfolded it. Her mouth fell open.

It was a crossword puzzle.

Crossword Grid

```
 1  2  3  4  ▓  5  6  7  8  ▓  9 10 11 12
13        14  ▓ 15        ▓ 16
17           ▓ 18        19
20        21  ▓ 22
 ▓ ▓ 23     ▓ 24        ▓ ▓ ▓
25 26 27     28        ▓ 29 30 31 32 33
34    ▓ 35     ▓ 36
37    38 39     ▓ 40
41           42     ▓ 43
44        ▓ 45     46 47
 ▓ ▓    48 49     50     ▓ ▓
51 52 53 54     ▓ 55        56 57 58
59           60  ▓ 61
62    ▓ 63        64
65    ▓ 66        67
```

ACROSS

1 Attire
5 Prickly seed covers
9 Afrikaner
13 Spring zodiac sign
15 ___ arms (angry)
16 BBs and bullets
17 Horizontal row in sudoku
18 Message part 1
20 Where Easy Street is?
22 Seeing the sun rise, say
23 "Yo!"
24 Gone by
25 Message part 2
29 Number of numbers in
   numbered row
34 Messenger ___
35 Bridge pro Culbertson
36 Place for an ace?
37 Gentlemanly reply
40 Garden seasoner
41 Goes on stage
42 Fannie or Ginnie follower
43 All-purpose truck, briefly
44 Cook one's goose?

45 Message part 3
48 The big picture?
50 "Get my drift?"
51 Like a system with equal gains and losses
55 Popular chocolate bar
59 Message part 4
61 "Sayonara!"
62 Parisian pig meat
63 Lake, canal, or city
64 Palm tree or nut
65 Kind of terrier
66 Jet-setters' jets, once
67 Clear the leaves

DOWN

1 Iron fishhook with handle
2 Diva's delivery
3 Diplomacy breakdown
4 "You ___!" ("Right!")
5 In use
6 Wire service inits.
7 Ceremony
8 Takes it from the top?
9 Lower California, familiarly
10 "Rubáiyát" poet
11 Olympic track champion Zatopek
12 ___-poly
14 Balks, as a horse
19 Rub the wrong way

21 Hyper, impatient ones
24 Practice a trade
25 Young chicken
26 Bridge bid, briefly
27 Jamaican in dreadlocks
28 With sudoku, address of house you went in
30 ". . . sat down beside ___"
31 Show with a medley
32 Mrs. Peron
33 Angler of morays
36 "Aw, c'mon!"
38 Enero, por ejemplo
39 One who makes a scene?
40 Cleveland cager, briefly
42 Nation that celebrates Cinco de Mayo: Abbr.
45 New parents, usually
46 Betty Ford Clinic program, e.g.
47 Birdseed holder
49 Zaps the sound
51 Whizzes
52 "Return of the Jedi" creature
53 "Marco Polo" star Calhoun
54 Enough, for some
55 Bullfight bravos
56 Naldi of the Ziegfeld Follies
57 Stink
58 The season to be jolly
60 Burning

"It isn't solved. How do you know it's a blackmail note?"
"We made a copy. We solved it."
"This is a copy?"
"This is the note. We solved the copy."

"Where is the copy?"

"It's gone."

"What did it say?"

"I don't remember. You'll have to solve it."

Cora snorted in exasperation. "Oh, for Pete's sake!" She looked to Sherry for help.

"Oh, go ahead and solve it, Cora. But not the original. I'll make a copy."

Sherry got up, took the puzzle, and went down the hall to her office.

Cora glared after her, then turned back to Michiko. "How'd your aunt get a blackmail note? She's in jail."

"It came to the motel where we're staying."

"You got a blackmail note at the motel?"

"It was under the door."

"So you took it to your aunt?"

"I told you. I made a *copy* and took it to my aunt. In the jail. She solved it and we destroyed it."

"In *general*, what did the puzzle say?"

"That someone knew what she did."

"What did she do?"

"Nothing."

"I don't understand."

"No. There was a sudoku with the puzzle." Michiko reached into her purse again, took out another folded piece of paper.

Cora unfolded it and found the sudoku.

6			1	5		8		4
			2					
		2		9				1
		8				4		6
1							3	2
9			7		6			
					9	6		
				3	7			
	5					9		

"You made a copy of this and she solved it?"

"A copy, yes. This is the original."

"So we have to copy this, too?"

"If you want to solve this one, I do not care if there's another."

"Neither do I. Where's a pencil?"

Cora found a pencil, sat down, and went to work on the sudoku. "Hmm. This is tricky. Did your aunt have trouble with it?"

"She had trouble with the crossword," Michiko said. "It is hard to deal with the English idiom."

"Uh huh," Cora said.

She finished the sudoku and passed it over.

6	9	7	1	5	3	8	2	4
4	1	5	2	7	8	3	6	9
3	8	2	6	9	4	5	7	1
5	7	8	3	2	1	4	9	6
1	4	6	9	8	5	7	3	2
9	2	3	7	4	6	1	5	8
2	3	4	5	1	9	6	8	7
8	6	9	4	3	7	2	1	5
7	5	1	8	6	2	9	4	3

"What does that tell you?"

"You need the crossword puzzle."

Sherry came back from the office, holding the puzzle. "Here you go," she said, folding it up and handing it to Michiko. "That's the original. I left the copy on the desk for you to solve, Cora."

"Thanks a heap. I just did the sudoku."

"What sudoku?"

"Take a look."

Cora heaved herself to her feet and padded down the hall to the office.

There on the desk, just as she expected, was the completed crossword puzzle. Sherry had whizzed through it in under five minutes. Cora couldn't have done it in under five days. She picked it up and looked it over.

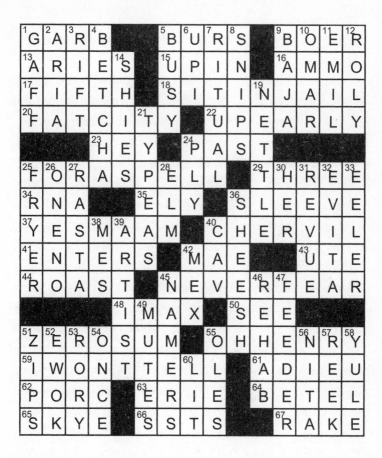

The theme answer was "Sit in jail for a spell. Never fear. I won't tell."

Cora snorted. That wasn't a blackmail note. Just a taunt.

Of course, in the note Cora got, the demands were hidden in the puzzle.

She scanned the puzzle for more clues.

She found 17 Across: Horizontal row in sudoku.

The answer was "Fifth."

29 Across: Number of numbers in numbered row.

The answer was "Three."

28 Down: With sudoku, address of house you went in.

The answer was "Elm."

Cora padded back down the hall. "All right, where's the damn sudoku? Ah, here we go." She snatched it up off the coffee table. "Let's see. Fifth row, first three numbers. One, four, six. So. Anyone happen to know who lives at 146 Elm Street? It wouldn't happen to be Sheila Preston, by any chance?"

"That is the one," Michiko said.

"You and your aunt figured that out, did you? When I asked you what the puzzle meant, and you said you couldn't remember, you were not being entirely frank with me, were you?"

"Cora," Sherry said warningly.

"No, no." Cora waggled her finger. "Just because she's young and pretty and Japanese doesn't mean she can get away with everything. Trust me, I know. I was young and pretty once, and I didn't. I certainly tried. Which is why I'm not being as hard on you as I should. The point is, you did all this fancy tapdancing around and made me solve a sudoku when you knew the answer all the time. And so did Minami. You guys figured it out while she was still in jail. Right? So, when she got out of jail she already knew she was being accused of going into 146 Elm. You picked her up from jail?"

"Yes."

"And brought her straight here?"

Michiko's eyes flicked.

Cora threw up her hands. "Teenagers! They lie so often and they're so bad at it. You didn't bring her straight here. Don't tell me you did. Don't even bother to try. Where'd you go first?"

"Back to the motel."

"And? There's an 'and,' isn't there?"

"What do you mean?"

"Were you with your aunt all the time, or did she take a little side excursion?"

"Excursion?"

"Did she leave you at the motel and go out?"

"She went to the drugstore. She had been in jail. There were some things she needed."

"How long was she gone?"

"I don't remember."

"It doesn't matter. I can figure it out. The police will know when they let her go. I know when she got to my house. I bet there's a chunk of time left in the middle. Good thing you can't write this, Aaron. She's just given us motive and opportunity."

Cora turned back to Michiko. "Does Becky Baldwin know this?"

"I don't know what my aunt has told her."

"Keep it that way. Don't ask Becky. Don't ask your aunt. Don't talk to anybody else. Luckily, you brought it to us first and we're all sworn to secrecy. Which makes us all accomplices after the fact, but, hey, what's a felony or two among friends? Well, congratulations. If you were trying to motivate me to save your aunt, you've done it. I've gotta get her off before we all wind up in jail."

Michiko said nothing, looked down at the floor.

"So," Cora said, "anything else you're not telling us?"

"Nothing else," Michiko said.

But she couldn't meet Cora's eyes.

Cora caught up with Dennis in the bar at the Country Kitchen.

"Hey, Dennis, how you doin'? What you havin'? Here, let me buy you a drink. Barkeep, a Diet Coke and whatever poison he's drinkin'."

Dennis, clearly disconcerted, didn't know how to respond. He forced a smile, said, "To what do I owe this honor?"

"Funny you should ask. You owe it to your keen powers of observation, your shrewd deductions, and your injudicious advances toward unfortunate adolescents."

"Huh?"

"You blew it, baby, and you blew it good. Got yourself in a heap of trouble. Luckily, Aunt Cora's here to get you out."

"I don't know what you're talking about."

"Excellent tack to take. Knowing what I was talking about

would be an admission of guilt. Ignorance is a much better op-tion. Ah, here's our drinks. Well, 'Bottoms up,' as they used to say in the sorority. As I recall, they weren't talking about drinking. Though they probably were. Drinking, I mean."

"Are you drunk?"

"Drunk with power. Drunk with knowledge. But alcohol? Haven't had a drop. Don't miss it as much as I used to. Even in a bar. So, you want me to tell you where you went wrong?"

"If you're going to lecture me, I don't want the drink."

"It's not a lecture. It's shrewd advice. The type your lawyer'd give you, if she wasn't representing everybody else. But don't tell her I said so. If Becky thought I was costing her business, there'd be hell to pay."

"Any time you'd like to get to the point."

"Boy, a bourbon doesn't buy you as much as it used to. I ex-pected at least a little civility."

"I think I'm gonna go."

"Making you nervous? That's not surprising, considering the fix you're in."

Dennis got up from his stool and started for the door.

"I know about the blackmail note."

Dennis stopped in his tracks. He didn't turn, but he didn't leave either. He just stood there.

Cora walked up behind him. "Where you made your big mis-take was running a bluff on the kid. It worked, sure, it was bound to work. And you know *she's* not going to the cops. But you didn't count on her coming to me. And while she may not be old enough and wise enough to make the connection, I had no problem.

"The connection, of course, is where did you get the idea? You're not bright enough to have come up with it yourself, so something must have put it in your head. Now what might that be? Only one thing I can think of. You got one, too. Wanna tell me about it?"

He turned around. "Now, look here."

"Yes?"

His eyes shifted.

"That's funny. You're outraged, but you can't think of anything to say that doesn't get you in deeper. Never fear, Cora's here. Let me walk you through this. Come over here where no one can eavesdrop and unburden yourself."

Cora steered Dennis over to a corner booth and sat him against the wall. "Good. See, no one can sneak up behind you. Keep your voice low, try not to fly into an indignant fury, and you'll do just fine. Now, tell me about the blackmail note."

"What makes you think there's a blackmail note?"

"What makes me think the sun rose? I see it in the sky. I don't wonder how it got there. I'm just glad it did."

"You're loopier than ever."

"Well, who wouldn't be? I got a Japanese counterpart on a bizarre book tour, doing a Jack Abbott bit."

"Who?"

"That's before your time? Good lord, where did the years go? Never mind. We're talking about you. You teased the little girl about her aunt getting a blackmail note. You're not smart enough to have thought of it yourself, which means you must have got one, which means you were there."

Dennis opened his mouth to speak.

"Not at Thelma Wilson's. At Sheila Preston's. Before the body was found. At least, before the body was reported. Thelma Wilson saw you go in."

"That's a lie!"

Cora made a face. "Oh. Bad line reading. That's not convincing at all. I know Thelma Wilson saw you go in. She told me so herself."

His eyes flicked.

Cora waved his reaction away. "Not in so many words. But she told me about your visit. After Minami was arrested. You went and interviewed her. I wondered why. Mrs. Wilson had already identified Minami. The police had taken Minami off to jail; there wasn't much more to learn. What did you want to know? I asked Thelma Wilson about it, and guess what? She couldn't come up with an answer. At least, not a good one. There seemed to be no purpose for your visit. But I knew there was. What could it possibly be? There was only one thing I could think of. You were at Sheila's house that day, and you wanted to know if Thelma Wilson had seen you go in."

Dennis said nothing and took a slug of his drink.

"So, what did the note say?"

"What note?"

"Dennis, Dennis, if you don't tell me about the note, then I gotta go to Chief Harper, and I don't wanna go to Chief Harper 'cause he'll just be mad that I know more than he does. Then he'll drag you in and interrogate you without me, in an attempt to know more than I do. Then Becky Baldwin will get involved, and she won't let you answer his questions. But she'll have a bunch of her own. Think about it. Who would you rather tell your story to? Me, Chief Harper, Becky Baldwin? Or your wife?"

His face fell.

Cora smiled. "Ooo. Surprise left jab stuns opponent, leaves him open to uppercut. Didn't see that coming, did you?"

"Are you having fun?"

"No, I'm really not. Come on, what did the note say?"

He glared at her for a moment. "It said, 'I know what you did.'"

"Is that all?"

"That's the gist of it."

"It didn't ask for money?"

"No. Why?"

"Why? Blackmail notes usually ask for money."

"This one didn't."

"What else did it say?"

"Nothing."

"Where is it?"

"It's gone."

"Oh?"

"I don't have it anymore."

"Why not?"

"I just don't."

"You just don't because you lost it? Because you turned it over to the police? Because you left it at the scene of the crime? Any time I hit one you like—"

"I destroyed it."

"Why?"

"I didn't want to get in trouble."

"That might have worked if you hadn't made a pass at the little girl."

"I didn't make a pass at her."

"You know what I mean. What else did the note say?"

"Nothing."

"It didn't ask you to come to see her?"

"No, why would it? I'd already been to see her."

"Yeah, but you hadn't admitted anything. You hadn't told and she hadn't asked. You were being accused. That changes things. I would think she'd want to see you."

"Well, you're wrong."

"And you conveniently destroyed the note so we can't prove any different."

"That's not why!"

"Nonetheless, that's the result."

"I can't help that. It's the truth. It's the whole truth. I told you everything I know. I kept my end of the bargain. Now, you going to the cops?"

Cora patted him on the cheek. "Absolutely not."

"Dennis got a blackmail note."

Chief Harper's scone stopped halfway to his lips. He lowered it reluctantly, looked over at Cora. "What?"

"He got a blackmail note. From Thelma Wilson. If I were you, I'd pick him up and sweat him."

"Are you kidding me?"

"Not at all. He'll probably deny it. He destroyed the note, and he swears he didn't go see her. At least on the day of the murder. Of course, he could be lying."

"Son of a bitch!"

"That's him, all right. If I were you, I'd haul him in. He's either gonna talk or call his lawyer. If he calls Becky Baldwin, that will put you in the perfect position to argue conflict of interest. Becky won't have a leg to stand on. Whether or not one client got a blackmail note from the victim has to have an impact on whether or not another client did the deed."

Harper put up his hand. "Hold on, hold on. Let me think about this." The move was clearly to allow him to eat his scone because that's what he did. He took a huge bite, washed it down with coffee. The world looked immediately brighter. He took another bite of scone.

"While you're eating, Chief, allow me to point out that any evidence connecting Minami to the crime is almost certainly manufactured. With so much evidence against Dennis, it's gonna be hard to convict her."

"Hang on a moment." Harper chewed and swallowed. "I've lost sight of your motivation in all this. Whose side are you on?"

"My own, of course."

"Of course. So what do you hope to gain by coming to me?"

"What do you mean? We've always worked together."

"Not this time. You've been playing me ever since this thing started. Giving Becky's clients advice. Giving Becky advice. Giving me advice. Until I don't know what to believe anymore."

"Chief, I wouldn't steer you wrong. Well, I might, but not in a way you could get hurt. This is a case with too many suspects, and they're all represented by Becky Baldwin. No one will talk to me. Someone's gotta talk to you. I'm hopin' if I give you a tip, you'll let me in on where it leads."

"That's all you want?"

"Absolutely."

Becky Baldwin slammed the door of her Honda and thundered up the path on high-heeled shoes, her blond hair bouncing around her neck like the mane of an angry lion.

Cora saw her coming and opened the door. "Come right in. You're just in time for tea."

"Damn it," Becky said, sweeping in the door. "How could you do that?"

"Do what?"

"You know what. You sicced Chief Harper onto Dennis."

"Is that what he says?"

"Don't get cute. You did it and you know it, and you cost me a client."

"Dennis?"

"No, not Dennis. I can't lose Dennis. I'm representing him with the probation board."

"Minami?"

"That's what Harper says."

"How can you quit Minami? She's up on a murder charge."

"The chief says I can't do both. And whose fault would that be?"

"I would say yours, for picking guilty clients."

"I'm not quitting Minami, and I'm not quitting Dennis, and now I got a hearing in front of Judge Hobbs to show cause why I should not be relieved as Minami's counsel due to a conflict of interest."

"That doesn't sound like fun."

"Damn it, Cora, why'd you do it? I thought we were friends."

"We *are* friends. But lately the friendship's been a little one-sided. You got me workin' on a case, and keeping me in the dark."

"So you decided to get back at me?"

"Don't be silly. I'm trying to save my own skin. You're not leveling with me. Harper's not leveling with me. Dennis certainly isn't, and you won't let me talk to Minami. It's a rather frustrating situation. Everyone I wanna talk to is either dead or your client."

"Why do you care?"

"Huh?"

"If Minami gets convicted, what's it to you? I thought she was your rival."

"She is my rival. That's the trouble. If I didn't know her at all, it would be fine. But she came here to pick a fight with me. If I let her take the fall for murder because it's none of my business, I'm gonna have this nagging doubt that I did it to get rid of a competitor."

"That's silly."

"Tell me about it. And the stupid thing is the woman's so obviously innocent. The whole thing's absurd. So, if you want me to help you, if you want me to help your client, for God's sake, tell me what's going on."

Becky flopped down on the couch, sighing. "Okay."

"Okay? Well, that wasn't so hard now, was it?" Cora cocked her head. "I'm listening."

"Thelma Wilson was blackmailing Minami."

Cora nodded. "With a crossword puzzle and a sudoku."

"You knew that?"

"Yesterday's news. Go on."

Becky blinked. "Go on? What do you mean, go on? That's the story. That's her motive. She was being blackmailed." Her eyes widened. "Good God. Did you tell Chief Harper?"

"None of his business."

"You're kidding."

"You want me to tell Chief Harper?"

"Of course not."

"Well, I didn't. So what are you griping about?"

"How did you know?"

Cora smiled. "I'm sorry. That's puzzle maker-client privilege. I'm afraid I can't say."

Becky frowned. "Damn it. You *are* trying to get back at me."

"Just kidding. Come on, I know about Minami's involvement in the Thelma Wilson murder. What's the deal with Sheila Preston?"

"You know the deal with Sheila Preston. It's the gospel according to Thelma Wilson. Which is what got Minami in jail in the first place. Which is what makes the whole thing so stupid. How could Thelma Wilson be blackmailing Minami by threatening to tell what she already told?"

"'Sit in jail for a spell. Never fear, I won't tell.' Along with

Sheila's address. I actually like it. It's a clever move on Thelma Wilson's part. It reveals no new information. But the implied threat is there: I know this, what else do I know? If the police were to intercept it and solve it, it wouldn't tell them a thing. Except to point the finger at Minami. Which has already been done. But anything that enforces the idea is gravy. On the other hand, there is nothing specific to point to Thelma Wilson. The police may know she sent it, but they can't prove it. 'Crossword puzzle? What crossword puzzle? I'm not the one who does crossword puzzles. You must be thinking of that Puzzle Lady person.'"

"You mean she wanted people to think you sent it?"

"I wouldn't go that far."

Becky's eyes narrowed suspiciously. "You *didn't* send it, did you?"

"Give me a break. Do you think I'm the type of person to plant evidence on your client?"

"No, of course not."

"I'm glad to hear it. Now, before we went off on a tangent, you were telling me what was going on. Thelma Wilson was blackmailing Minami. And . . . ?"

"Someone else killed Thelma Wilson, framed Minami with a sudoku, and she wound up in jail."

"That's not what I meant and you know it. Thelma Wilson figured Minami for the murder of Sheila Preston. Because Minami came to see her twice. She went to the house, ran away, got her niece, and came back. Thelma Wilson told the police, that's what got Minami on the hook. I can't believe Minami killed Sheila Preston, though stranger things have happened. If she didn't kill her, what did she do? She came to the house, ran away, came back with her niece. Why?"

"The motivation doesn't matter. What's important is what she did."

"The motivation doesn't matter?" Cora said incredulously. "You're an attorney and you claim her motivation doesn't matter?"

"Not in this case. Not when it's incidental. Not when it has nothing to do with the crime. Suppose she forgot her purse? Suppose she remembered she had a doctor's appointment? Suppose Sheila said, 'I'm really busy, could you come back in half an hour?' "

"You're claiming that when Minami called on her, Sheila was alive?"

"I'm claiming nothing of the sort. I'm giving you examples."

"They're *bad* examples. They have nothing to do with real life."

"I can't help that. I came here in the spirt of cooperation."

"Cooperation, hell. You came here to gripe. You got too many clients, and they're giving you a hard time, and you're blaming me. Maybe I got it coming, but let's not pretend that's why you're here. You're in a sticky situation and you need my help. Hell, you need anybody's help. And you're willing to do whatever you have to do to get it. Except level with me. On issues you claim are extraneous." Cora took a breath. "So. Dennis told you Chief Harper was hassling him?"

"That's right. Because of you."

"And because he got a blackmail note."

Becky blinked. "What?"

"Dennis didn't tell you that?" Cora grinned. "Glad I could be of help."

Aaron Grant held up a bone from his rack of lamb.

"Let me be sure I got this straight. Dennis got a blackmail note from Thelma Wilson?"

"That's right."

"But it wasn't a crossword puzzle."

"He's not a puzzle person. Thelma Wilson knew that. She was a good judge of character."

"What's the point of blackmailing Dennis?"

Cora shrugged. "What's the point of blackmailing Minami? It wasn't the money. The woman got off on power. She loved to play "I got a secret" and make people jump through hoops. She played it on Minami. She played it on Dennis. She played it on me. She didn't *really* know anything, but she wanted people to think she did."

"How could she play it on Dennis? What made her think blackmailing Dennis might work?"

"He's that type of guy."

"No, I mean what did she have on Dennis? She didn't send him the note on a whim. She had to have reason to believe he'd done something he could be blackmailed about."

"Naturally."

"So, what was it?"

"She probably saw him go into the house."

"What makes you think that?"

"It's a logical inference."

"Come on, Cora. What makes you think that?"

"Because Dennis went into the house."

"You know that for a fact?"

"You can take it to the bank."

"You saw him go into the house?"

"I refuse to answer on the grounds an answer might wind up in the morning paper."

"Is it true?"

"Relax. Eat your rack of lamb. You worked hard enough on it."

"It took five minutes."

"It took five minutes in the frying pan. You had to prepare the bread crumbs and spices, you had to put it in the oven, take it out at the right time, and God knows what else. And it's absolutely perfect. I mean, just taste that rack of lamb."

"Uh oh. You never babble like that unless you're guilty. That's the most you've said about cooking in three years. What did you do now? More to the point, what did you do then?"

"If I saw Dennis go into Shelia Preston's house right before I went into Sheila Preston's house, that would be a hell of a thing to admit in front of a newspaper reporter, wouldn't it?"

"You're talking about me as if I weren't here," Aaron said.

"Not really," Cora corrected. "We're talking about you as if you were here but were rendered impotent by your current marriage." She frowned. "Seems to me I had a husband like that. Can't remember his name. The point is, Dennis was vulnerable, Thelma Wilson ran a bluff on him. Thelma Wilson had no idea who killed Sheila Preston, but she had a whole bunch of suspects. So she ran a bluff on all of them to see if she'd get a bite. Unfortunately, she did."

The case came on.

Cora snatched up the remote and clicked the TV off MUTE.

Rick Reed stood in front of the Bakerhaven Police Station. "The murder of Thelma Wilson took a bizarre turn this afternoon with the arrest of Dennis Pride. A somewhat unusual move on the part of Bakerhaven Police Chief Dale Harper, seeing as how he already has a suspect in jail for the crime. There is no suggestion that the two suspects were acting together as part of a criminal conspiracy. The police have what would seem to be an embarrassment of riches. It is usually hard enough to find one guilty-looking suspect, let alone two.

"Mr. Pride's attorney, Rebecca Baldwin, declined comment, partly due to the fact that she is also the attorney for the other suspect, Minami, the Sudoku Lady. But Minami's agent, Irving Swartzman, mocked the situation."

Swartzman, clad in a pin-striped zoot suit, smiled and scoffed. "The second arrest merely shows to what ridiculous lengths the police will go in an attempt to clear this crime. They have no idea what really happened, in light of which, keeping the Sudoku Lady in jail is a blatant miscarriage of justice. The Sudoku Lady did not come all the way from Japan to kill a stranger but merely to promote her book."

Once again, Swartzman held it up.

"I'm going to kill him," Cora said.

"Can I quote you on that if he winds up dead?" Aaron asked.

"It's ridiculous. The woman's doing almost as well as I am, and she's in jail and her book isn't even out yet."

Sherry looked up from the computer. "Actually . . ."

"What, actually?" Cora said.

"Her book is forty-two."

"On the puzzle books list?"

"On the Amazon.com list."

Cora's mouth fell open. "On the whole damn list?"

"Don't get excited."

"Wait till she gets convicted of this crime." Cora fumed. "We'll see what comfort her book sales are to her then."

"Cora, this is unlike you."

"Of course it is. Don't quote me in the paper."

"I haven't heard a quote yet I can use," Aaron said.

"Was that the doorbell?" Cora said.

It was. Buddy gave up his rack-of-lamb vigil to greet the intruder, perhaps in the hope of a reward.

"Who comes at dinnertime?" Cora said, as Sherry went to the door.

"The police," Aaron said.

"Bite your tongue."

Sherry ushered in Michiko.

Cora smiled. "Ah, déjà vu! Minami's agent appears on televison, Minami's niece appears at our door. What is it this time, another sudoku?"

"I must talk to you alone."

"I like it! Smacks of intrigue." Cora jerked her thumb in a take-a-hike gesture. "Okay, the rest of you guys, beat it."

"What?" Aaron said.

"She's joking," Sherry said. "Come on, Aaron, lighten up."

"Let's see, where can I take her? How about out back at the picnic table. No one can hear us, and I can smoke. Come on, kid. Let's leave this stodgy old married couple alone."

Cora ushered Michiko through the kitchen and out the back door. It was still light out, but there was a chill in the air. Cora pulled her sweater around her shoulders and asked, "Are you okay?" Michiko gave her a blank look. "What am I talking about? You're a teenager. Of course you're okay."

"Why do you talk like that?"

"Like what?"

"You are—what is the word?—you are not polite. You say whatever you want to say."

"Well, isn't that more convenient?"

"It is not respectful."

Cora laughed. "That's funny. You're scolding me for behaving like a bratty teenager." She added quickly, "No, of course not, of course not, you're not doing that. It would not be respectful. You only act that way toward your own relatives."

Cora flopped her drawstring purse down on the wooden picnic table, pulled out her cigarettes, and lit one. "Don't smoke. It's a bad habit and you don't want to get into it."

"Of course not."

Cora shook her head. "Of course not. Different generation. I wish we'd known enough to say 'of course not.' Now it's my one remaining vice. That and the occasional predatory male."

"I am Japanese. It is hard to understand you."

"You get the gist." Cora took a deep drag, blew it out. "So, what'd you want to tell me?"

"Minami is very proud."

"This may surprise you, but that isn't much of a revelation."

"It is important to consider."

"Why?"

"It is why she is in jail."

"Forgive me, but that's not entirely clear."

"I'm sorry. This is difficult for me. I am not sure how to say this. I feel I am betraying my aunt."

"Your aunt is in jail on a murder rap. Unless you're telling me she did it, you're not betraying her—you're trying to get her out."

"Yes, but—"

"There's always a but." Cora laughed. "At least there always was with Melvin. Big fan of Sir Mix-a-Lot."

"What?"

"Sorry. I keep forgetting how young you are. You probably weren't born yet. Go on."

"What I am about to say is for your ears only."

"Ah! American idiom! I love it!"

"I do not wish it to be known. If you cannot agree to that, I will not tell you. Do you agree to that?"

"You trust my word?"

"Your word is not good?"

"My word is good as gold. You can take it to the bank. But you don't know that. You're taking me on faith."

"I know, but I must do something." Michiko frowned and squinted at Cora sideways. "You do not wish me to tell you?"

"I wish you to tell me everything. And I want to go about getting your aunt out of jail. But I don't want you to tell me your aunt's broken the law and expect me to cover it up. I am not an attorney. I have no professional privileges. I would be guilty of conspiring to conceal a crime."

"It is not that."

"What is it then?"

Michiko took a breath. She looked down, set her jaw, then looked back up. "Minami cannot do sudoku."

Cora gasped. "What?"

"She is no good at it. She has no ability. She cannot construct them. She cannot solve them. She is no good at math. I construct all the puzzles. I do all the math. That is why I am on the trip. Not to be an interpreter but to solve the sudoku for her so no one will find out."

"Oh. My. God."

"You will not tell?"

"I will not tell." Cora shook her head. "Believe me, I'm just trying to adjust to the situation. So. The Sudoku Lady is a big fat fraud."

"That is not nice."

"And she was pissed my book sold better? I *wrote* my book."

"You are angry."

"I am not angry. I am shocked, *shocked* to find she doesn't construct her own sudoku. But I am not angry. I am broadminded, I am generous. I am forgiving. I am willing to live and let live. Just because your aunt is a fraud is no reason she should go to jail for murder." Cora's eyes opened wider. "Unless she killed someone who was going to expose her as a fraud."

"That is not true!"

"No?"

"It is ridiculous. My aunt would never do such a thing."

"Oh? You said she was very proud. She might kill to save her reputation."

"Stop! Stop! That is so stupid! You will not listen! You do not understand!"

There were tears in the girl's eyes. Cora took pity on her and stopped the harangue. "Okay, you tell me what happened."

"I do not know what happened. I mean, I do not know who killed those people. I just know it was not my aunt. She is in jail because she will not explain, and she will not explain because she can't do sudoku and she doesn't want anyone to know."

"Can't explain what?"

"Coming back to the house. That is what got her in trouble. That awful woman saw her come back to the house. Do you not see what happened? Minami came to the house. She found a woman dead. She found a sudoku. She could not do the sudoku. She knew the police would ask her to solve it. She could not solve it. She ran to get me."

"Oh, for goodness' sake."

"So, she cannot explain, and she must stay in jail." Michiko heaved a sigh. "It is not fair. It is just not fair. She is not good at puzzles. But she is good at crime. If she were not in jail, she would solve the murder and clear her name."

"Oh, dear."

"It is so frustrating. Then the police let her go, and what happens? That awful woman is killed. With a sudoku. It is so stupid. The sudoku proves she *didn't* do it. But no one knows it, and she will not tell. So she sits in jail. All because of a stupid sudoku she cannot solve."

"That is certainly ironic."

Michiko's head snapped up. Her eyes flashed. "Are you mocking me?"

"No, not at all. It really is ironic."

"So you must help. It is up to you. Only you can save her now. You are very smart, and you solve crime in your country as my aunt does in mine. You must solve this one. You must prove my aunt is innocent. Without betraying her secret."

"How am I going to do that?"

"You must find the killer."

"Oh, is that all?"

"You are mocking again?"

"Not you. Just your ideas. You act like it's easy to find a killer. It's damn hard. Even when your chief suspects are cooperating with the police."

"Yes, but you are very smart, and you know things that they do not know. Valuable clues."

"Yeah? Like what?"

"The sudoku."

"What sudoku?"

"The one in the awful woman's house."

"Oh."

"Have you noticed anything about it?"

"I barely noticed it at all. Trust me, it's not important."

"Oh, but it is."

"What?"

"The other sudoku—the one my aunt went and got me to solve—was a challenging sudoku. Not impossible but moderately difficult. But this sudoku was very easy. Like the ones in your book."

Cora felt a chill. Did the girl suspect her? "Excuse me?"

"Oh! I did not mean to insult you. But some of your puzzles are very easy. You know what I mean?"

"No, I don't. Some puzzles are easy. Some puzzles are hard. So what?"

"It's a clue. A valuable clue. If my aunt was talking, she could point that out and give the police a lead."

"I don't think so."

"Right. She could not. But you could. You could point out it was a much easier puzzle than the other one."

"I could, but why should I? It doesn't mean anything."

"How do you know? It could be important. It could mean that sudoku was left by a different person than whoever left the other sudoku."

"Oh, for goodness' sake."

Michiko made a face. "You dismiss my ideas because I am a child. Just because I am young does not mean I am not smart."

"Yes, yes, you're smart; your ideas are good. But the sudoku doesn't mean anything. Don't go wasting your time."

"It is not *my* time. It is the police—"

Cora waved her objections away. "Yes, yes, I know what you want. I'll do what I can."

"You'll go to the police?"

"You want me to tell the police?"

"About the sudoku. Not about my aunt."

"I know what you mean."

"You will do it? You will tell the police?"

"That's not going to thrill them much."

"But you will try?"

Cora sighed. "Look, kid. I'm going to try to get your aunt off. I'm not going to do it your way. If you want to do it your way, you don't need me. But that's okay with you, right, because you don't care as long as your aunt gets out of jail."

"But you will get her out of jail?"

"I'm not promising anything. I'm saying I will try."

Michiko looked concerned. "You won't let my aunt know I told you about her?"

Cora smiled. "Trust me."

Chapter

45

"I hear you're a big fat phony."

Minami looked up from her prison cot. "What did you say?"

"You heard me. Big deal Sudoku Lady. What's two plus two?"

"I don't understand. What are you talking about?"

"Take a wild guess." Cora whipped out a sheet of paper. "I got a sudoku here I need solved. You wanna do it?"

"I am not going to help you."

"You couldn't if you wanted to, you big fat phony."

"I am not fat."

Cora laughed. "You realize that's funny? Denying the fat part. Okay, you skinny little phony."

"What are you saying?"

"You know damn well what I'm saying. Here you are, so upset about whose book sells more, and you can't even do sudoku."

"Who says I cannot?"

"*I* say you cannot. Lucky for you, I'm saying it in here instead of on TV. But it happens to be true. You're an impostor. A charlatan. Hell, you're the Milli Vanilli of sudoku."

"Milli what?"

"Damn. One of my best lines, and you don't get the reference. You're no more the Sudoku Lady than you are the Wizard of Oz. You get that reference? 'Pay no attention to that man behind the curtain?'"

"Why are you doing this?"

"You wouldn't believe what a joy it is. After how smugly you tried to lord it over. And you're a big fat—excuse me—skinny little fraud."

"So. Michiko told on me."

Cora smiled. "Ah. American idiom. You can do it just fine when you want to. Your niece didn't tell on you. You niece came to your rescue. In the nick of time, believe me. Because things don't look too good. The police don't have a clue. They're all off on the wrong scent. This crime is not going to get solved, and you're going to rot in jail. It may be goosing your book sales, but it can't be doing much for your social life."

Minami took a breath. "Why are you here?"

"That's not the question you want to ask, is it? You want to ask am I going to expose you? But you don't wanna ask, because you don't want to put yourself in my power. Guess what? You're in it already. If I blab, you're toast. Relax. Cool your jets. I'm not gonna do that. What I'm gonna do is, I'm gonna sit down with you, and between the two of us, we're gonna figure a way out of this mess. After that, we'll go our separate ways and we won't bother each other again. Do we have a deal?"

Minami blinked. "What?"

"We gotta make a deal. It's important that we do before this goes any further. Tell you why. I got a confession of my own to make. And when you hear it, you're gonna be mad. And you're gonna wanna tell someone. But you can't do it. Any more than I can tell people about you. So, we can work together, or you can sit here till you rot and hope I keep my mouth shut. It doesn't sound like fun to me, but if you want to, you can. Or we can play *I've Got a Secret*. Wanna know my secret?"

"Yes."

"Make a deal and I'll tell you. Do we have a deal?"

"Yes."

Cora told her.

Chief Harper wasn't happy. "She has to be here?"

"Yes."

"Her lawyer should be present."

"Why?"

"Anything she says without counsel is inadmissible."

"She's not going to say anything."

"Then why does she have to be here?"

"Trust me, she does."

"Then Becky needs to be here."

"I warn you, it's going to be a problem."

"Not as much problem as if she isn't."

"Fine. Call Becky and get her over here."

"What do I tell her?"

"Tell her you're interrogating two suspects in the murder."

"They're not suspects."

"If you tell her they're suspects, you'll make her happy."

"Cora."

"You want her client present at an interrogation. She's not going to answer questions; she's just going to watch. Does Becky want to be there?"

"What if she objects to the whole thing?"

"I'll take her out in the woodshed and beat the crap out of her."

"That'll look bad in court."

"It won't be in court. It'll be in the woodshed. Come on, Chief, give Becky a call. If she agrees, no problem."

"What if she doesn't agree?"

"Then we'll think of something else. But I bet she does."

It was a safe bet. Cora and Becky had already discussed the plan. Becky didn't think Chief Harper would go for it, but Cora figured she could finesse him by pretending she didn't want Becky there and getting the chief to call her.

She figured right. Half an hour later, Minami, Becky, Cora, Chief Harper, and the two widowers, Jason Fielding and Steve Preston, were all jammed into the interrogation room.

Chief Harper cleared his throat. "I realize this is somewhat irregular, but we have some matters to clear up. Miss Felton has some questions. She wants the defendant here while she asks them."

"Why?" Steve Preston said. "Why do I have to sit here with her? She killed my wife."

"That's what we want to determine," Cora said. "There seems to be some doubt about that. Not in the eyes of the police, you understand. But I'd like to be satisfied. And I'm not. I have something to discuss. And I think she should hear it. And if you wanna know who killed your wife, I'd think you'd wanna hear it, too."

"Hear what?" Steve Preston said. "What in the world are you talking about?"

"From the very beginning we've had a problem with this case. When Ida Fielding was killed, her husband was in jail. There is no doubt about that. He was arrested in a bar fight, taken to jail, and locked in a cell. He was still there when she was discovered dead. She was alive when he was arrested; she was dead when he was released. There is no way he could have done it."

Cora turned to Steve Preston. "Your wife, same thing. She was killed while you were at work. In Manhattan, no less. A half a dozen co-workers can place you miles from the scene of the crime. Not quite as good as being in jail, but damn near. For all practical purposes, you couldn't possibly have done it."

Cora shook her head. "Which was really annoying. Particularly with rumors of infidelity flying about."

"Hey!"

"Damn you!"

Cora put up her hands. "Yes, yes, I know, your wives are innocent; you're outraged, yada, yada, yada. But the point is, you guys have perfect alibis."

"That's right," Jason said. "So why are we here? Why do we have to put up with this?"

"Strangers on a Train."

Steve Preston frowned and said, "What?"

But Jason Fielding's mouth fell open.

Cora smiled. "I'm glad at least one of you caught the reference."

Jason scowled. "Yes, I know what you mean. It's a Hitchcock movie. About two men who kill each other's wives. Is that what you think happened here?"

"I don't know. You're pretty quick to jump on the theory."

"What do you mean, 'jump on it'? I happen to be a film buff.

I know every Alfred Hitchcock movie. The minute you mention *Strangers on a Train*, I know exactly what you're getting at."

"What the hell is she talking about?"

"She thinks we killed each other's wives. Like in the movie. Because we have perfect alibis. I couldn't have killed my wife; you couldn't have killed yours. We could have killed each other's."

"Why?"

"I don't know. She hasn't told me. Why would we do that?"

"You tell me."

"Tell you what? I don't know what you're talking about."

"He sounds sincere. What do you think, Minami? Is this man a killer?"

"Hang on," Becky said. "I can't have you questioning my client."

Cora looked surprised. "I thought we had an agreement here."

"Sorry. I can't let you question her."

"Not even on the guilt of a third party?

"*Especially* on the guilt of a third party."

"How come?"

"It opens the door. What if you asked her about Dennis?"

"Why would I do that?"

"I know you. You're apt to do anything."

"I promise I won't ask her about Dennis." Cora turned to Chief Harper. "Chief, can we get Dennis in here?"

"What?" Becky exclaimed.

"You don't want me to ask her about Dennis, then I'll ask Dennis about her."

"Wait a minute, wait a minute," Chief Harper said. "I don't like the way this is going."

"This is all unofficial," Cora said. "No one's getting hurt."

"Except me, when the prosecutor finds out."

"So, ask him," Cora said.

"What?

"Call him up, ask him if he minds."

"That's not a great idea," Becky said.

"Oh?" Harper said. "And why not?"

"It just isn't."

Cora grinned. "Sorry, Becky. I hate to hang you out to dry, but I'm afraid it can't be helped. We have these crimes to clear up."

She cocked her head at the chief. "Call Ratface."

Chapter

4 7

Henry Firth had a thin mustache and a twitchy little nose, which always reminded Cora of a rat. Of course, the fact that the Baker-haven prosecutor was usually on the other side didn't help; nor did the fact that he was often thoroughly exasperated with her.

"So," he said ironically to Chief Harper, "let me be sure I've got this straight. You brought the two husbands here in order to accuse them of killing each other's wives in front of the defendant and her attorney, just in case she needed a good theory to argue in front of the jury during the trial. When that didn't pan out—and lord knows I can't imagine why it didn't—you proposed bringing in the other suspect in the case, who in your infinite wisdom you managed to arrest just in case convicting the defendant was going to be a little too easy. You only thought to bring me in when the defense attorney herself dug in her heels at this rather bizarre suggestion, which surpasseth the bounds of human understanding."

"You're really good when you're angry," Cora said. "You're not too keen at presenting facts, but you can do elaborate sarcasm along with the best of them."

"I'd advise you to hold your tongue," Henry Firth said. "You're not an attorney, so this isn't your fault. But I would imagine that is the *only* reason this isn't your fault. This whole thing just smacks of Cora Felton."

Cora grimaced. "You're better with sarcasm. Direct accusation is tougher to pull off. You need to work on your delivery."

Firth turned to Chief Harper. "Can you keep her quiet?"

"How?"

"Good point. Ms. Baldwin, this is to a large part your fault. As attorney for the defendant, you should never have agreed to this arrangement."

"I don't see why not," Becky said. "We were having fun until you showed up."

"I wouldn't take this lightly, young lady. There is some question as to the eligibility of your representation. The arrest of Mr. Pride has complicated the situation significantly. You are the attorney handling his probation, thus his attorney of record. His interests in this case are in direct conflict with those of the defendant. If you wish to continue to represent him, then you cannot represent her. It's a direct conflict of interest."

"I disagree."

"It's not your place to disagree. It's your place to obey the law."

"Oh, that sounds good," Cora said. "It's meaningless, of course, but it *sounds* good."

"We'll see how meaningless it is. Now, let's apologize to these two gentlemen for putting them through this charade and send them on their way."

"You mean they're not going to see Dennis Pride?" Cora said.

"No, they're not going to see Dennis Pride. They're going home, the defendant's going back to jail, Chief Harper's going back to work. By which I mean his actual work and not this type of tomfoolery. And Ms. Baldwin's going before Judge Hobbs to show cause why she should not be removed as counsel due to a conflict of interest." Henry Firth's ratty nose twitched. "How does *that* sound?"

Cora smiled. "Sounds like fun."

Judge Hobbs cleared his throat. "This is the time scheduled for the hearing to show cause why Ms. Baldwin should not be removed from representation of her client due to a conflict of interest." The elderly jurist looked around the courtroom. "This is not a public proceeding. I was not aware there would be spectators."

Henry Firth was on his feet, his nose twitching. "They are not spectators, Your Honor. They are interested parties."

"I see," Judge Hobbs said dryly. "That would include the camera crew from Channel 8 News?"

"They're interested, Your Honor."

"I'll bet they are," the judge muttered. He picked up a paper from the bench. "Ms. Baldwin, it is alleged that you are representing two clients, Minami and Dennis Pride, with conflicting interests in the murder case of Thelma Wilson and that of Sheila Preston. Are you prepared to show that they are not?"

"I am not the one making the claim, Your Honor. If the district attorney has that theory, he's certainly free to voice it."

Judge Hobbs digested that. Didn't like it. He turned to Henry Firth. "What's the basis of this conflict of interest?"

"What's the basis? Three people have been killed. Her client, Minami, is charged with at least one of their deaths. Her other client, Dennis Pride, was sent a blackmail note by that very decedent. We have two people with strong, separate motives for killing the victim, and she's representing both of them."

Becky smiled. "Is it the prosecutor's contention that either client is equally likely to have committed the crime?"

Judge Hobbs banged the gavel. "That will do. We're not here for verbal sparring. As for you, young lady, I'm not at all happy to have you speak in your own behalf. You're already representing two clients. It would seem your workload was rather full."

"I have no problem with representing myself, Your Honor."

"Well, I do. You know the old adage about a lawyer serving in that capacity having a fool for a client. We have enough problems with conflict of interest without interjecting your own."

"I think I can remain impartial, Your Honor."

"Well, I'm going to relieve you of that responsibility. Please obtain outside counsel."

"Very well, Your Honor. In that case, I am going to ask Miss Cora Felton to represent me."

The Puzzle Lady, decked out in a full-length tweed overcoat, rose from the second row of the gallery and came forward.

Henry Firth's mouth fell open. "Your Honor, I object. She's not an attorney."

"No, Your Honor," Becky said. "Miss Felton is here as amicus curiae. As a friend of the court, she has agreed to act in my behalf."

"Well, she's not going to," Judge Hobbs ruled. "She's not an attorney."

"No, but I am, Your Honor."

"That doesn't matter," Henry Firth sputtered.

"Oh, pooh." Cora dismissed the prosecutor with a wave of her hand and made her way to Becky's table. "This isn't a trial, for goodness' sake. I'm not representing the defendant. Though, I must say, I'd certainly like to. The issue right now is whether this young woman has a right to practice law. Granted, the judicial system tends to be seen as an old boy's club, and it's only lately that women have managed to gain any foothold at all. I find it sad that the minute the brightest and the best begins to make a name for herself, the old boys in charge endeavor to strip her of her clients."

Judge Hobbs banged the gavel. "How dare you!"

"I apologize for the word 'old,' Your Honor. I don't like it much myself. But look what's happening here. You all gang up on this gal, say she can't have her client. When she objects, you tell her she's not allowed to speak for herself, she has to get an outside attorney. There don't happen to be any in this town, so she's going to have to go to New York, which is going to take some time. Are you willing to give her a continuance until next week to allow her to obtain outside counsel? During which time, of course, she would retain both clients."

District Attorney Henry Firth almost fell over himself spouting objections.

Judge Hobbs again banged the gavel. "Sit down, Mr. Firth. The court takes note of your unwillingness to stipulate."

"You see, Your Honor," Cora said, "we are sort of at an impasse.

This is something that should be cleared up now. I would think that you, as a long-time proponent of equal rights, would want to see that women have every opportunity to have the same advantages as the men in the community." She stole a look at the TV cameras. "Because, if there is one thing we are in Bakerhaven, Connecticut, it is modern, progressive, and fairminded. We're not some bigoted, close-minded, small town community, clinging to antiquated perceptions and hopelessly behind the times. Are we, Your Honor?"

Judge Hobbs opened his mouth. Closed it again. Looked at the TV cameras. Wondered what he could possibly say that wouldn't leave him looking like a moron. It didn't help his disposition to realize that his taking so long to answer was creating exactly that impression. "There is no cause for speeches. Nor is there cause for any theatrics. We have a simple situation here, easily resolved. If you want to speak for Ms. Baldwin, feel free. Though I hope you won't expect special treatment in light of your lack of courtroom experience."

"Of course not. In Your Honor's courtroom, I would expect simple logic to prevail."

"Good. You can start by removing that coat."

"I beg your pardon?"

"You are wearing an overcoat in my courtroom. It is not proper attire. Take it off."

"Really, Your Honor, this is just what I was talking about. Would you object to the way a *male* attorney was dressed?"

"I would if he was wearing a trench coat. Take it off."

"I'd rather not, Your Honor."

"Why? It's not cold. Do you contend that you are cold in my courtroom?"

"No, Your Honor."

"Then there's no reason for that overcoat."

"Actually, there is, Your Honor."

"Oh? And what is that?"

"I would prefer not to say. I have personal reasons for wearing this coat. I do not wish to state them in open court. Commanding me to do so is invading my privacy."

Judge Hobbs stared at her, stymied.

"Oh, Your Honor," Henry Firth said. "We are getting far afield. This is a simple matter of conflict of interest. The facts are indisputable. I would suggest that these theatrics are merely a distraction to keep us from our purpose."

"Well, that's not going to happen. Miss Felton, we shall address the matter of your attire later in my chambers. At which time I will decide whether your refusal to comply with my simple request should not be construed as contempt of court."

Cora smiled. "Thank you, Your Honor."

There was a ripple of laughter in the courtroom. Judge Hobbs silenced it with his gavel. "Mr. Firth, make your case."

"I already did."

"What?"

"Minami. Dennis Pride. They have conflicting interests in the murder of Thelma Wilson, and she represents them both."

"Thank you. That's concise, to the point, and would seem to be definitive. Miss Felton, what do you say to that?"

"I would have to agree, Your Honor. I think the prosecutor put it very well."

"Is he correct?"

"Very rarely, Your Honor. In Vegas you could probably make a living asking his opinion and betting the other way."

"There is no cause for levity. People are dead."

"Exactly. Which is why people are suspected and Becky Baldwin is defending them."

"I think we all understand the situation. How do you resolve the conflict of interest?"

"I don't think it exists."

Henry Firth lunged to his feet.

"I know the district attorney thinks that it does, but he can't prove it. In fact, the minute he examines the case with any reasonable degree of scrutiny, I think he will see that the interests of the two clients in question are identical and complement each other, rather than raising any conflict."

"That is your contention?" Henry Firth said.

"Absolutely," Cora told him.

The prosecutor smiled. "Well, Your Honor. It would seem to me that the burden of proof has been shifted onto her."

"I think so, too," Judge Hobbs said. He added dryly, "Though I must say, I am not as thrilled about it as you are. Miss Felton, you claim the interests of Dennis Pride and Minami are identical?"

"Yes, Your Honor."

"Do you have any evidence to back up that assertion?"

"Of course."

Judge Hobbs nodded in weary resignation. "Very well. Make your case."

Cora Felton strode to the middle of the courtroom. She was quite a striking figure in the long tweed coat. "I take it you will not be persuaded by my own assurance?"

"I most certainly will not."

"Then I will have to call witnesses. Let's start with Chief Harper. He's certainly an interested party."

Surprised and none too pleased, Chief Harper took the stand.

"You want to swear him in, Your Honor, or can we assume he's going to tell the truth?"

"Do you intend to call other witnesses?"

"Yes, Your Honor."

"Can the same be said of them?"

"You mean can I vouch for their veracity? Not in every case."

"Then I'm not going to let you single out which ones to believe. Swear him in."

"Suits me, Your Honor."

Cora waited while the chief was sworn in, then began her questioning. "Chief Harper, you've just sworn to tell the truth."

"Yes, I have."

"Were you going to tell it anyway?"

"Objection," Henry Firth said. "What is the point of this inquiry?"

"I was willing to take him at his word," Cora said. "Since that didn't happen, I think he should be allowed to clear his good name."

"Oh, Your Honor. Could we put an end to these manipulative theatrics?"

"We can. It is hereby directed that we do. Miss Felton, you are trying the patience of the court. Please get to the point."

"Chief Harper, you arrested the suspect, Minami, the Sudoku Lady, on suspicion of murder?"

"Yes, I did."

"Did you arrest her on more than one occasion?"

"Yes."

"For the same crime?"

"No. For two separate crimes. The murder of Sheila Preston and the murder of Thelma Wilson."

"How did that come to happen?"

"I arrested her for the murder of Sheila Preston on the testimony of the eyewitness, Thelma Wilson."

"Was that the only evidence against her?"

"Objection! Miss Felton is a friend of the defense counsel. This is a blatant attempt to get the prosecution to reveal its case."

"So what?"

"What do you mean, 'So what?' It's improper."

"Why? Does your whole case revolve around surprising the defendant? Are you afraid you can't convict her on the facts alone?"

Judge Hobbs banged the gavel. "That will do. Miss Felton, I am aware that you have a facility with words. But that does not allow you to circumvent proper legal procedure. It is not proper to ask a police officer to outline the prosecutor's case."

"Surely I'm allowed to ask what evidence he arrested her on."

"Go ahead. But don't overstep your bounds."

"Chief Harper, did you arrest Minami solely on the testimony of Thelma Wilson?"

"I arrested her on the grounds that she left the murder scene and then returned to it. And by the fact that a sudoku was found on the body. She is, after all, the Sudoku Lady."

"And why did you arrest her for the murder of Thelma Wilson?"

"Thelma Wilson was the chief witness against her. No sooner was she released from jail than Thelma Wilson was killed. Once again, a sudoku was found next to the body."

"Thank you, Chief. That's all."

"Would the prosecutor care to cross-examine?"

"There's no need, Your Honor. Miss Felton is making my case for me. She's just proven beyond a shadow of a doubt that the defendant is in need of counsel."

"There's no need for a speech," Judge Hobbs said irritably. "The court notes you decline to cross-examine. Chief Harper, you may step down. Miss Felton, call your next witness."

"That's a problem, Your Honor. I'd like to call Thelma Wilson. She could clear this right up. Unfortunately, she's dead."

"What a shame the defendant happened to kill the very person who could have cleared her," Henry Firth said sarcastically.

Judge Hobbs banged the gavel. "That will do. Would you like to call anyone who's still living?"

"Call Dennis Pride."

"Objection, Your Honor."

"On what grounds?"

"Dennis Pride is a suspect in this investigation. As such, he needs to be represented by counsel."

"There she sits."

"He *can't* be represented by her. It's a conflict of interest."

Cora waggled her fingers. "Sorry. You can't use that argument. That is yet to be determined. Or we wouldn't be here."

Dennis Pride stepped up to the witness stand, with very much of the star persona he affected in his role as the lead singer of his band—cocky, arrogant, self-assured. "No problem, Your Honor. I waive my right to counsel at this hearing. I have nothing to fear and nothing to hide. I am just as eager to get this straightened out as anyone."

"Well, that's a refreshing attitude," Judge Hobbs said.

"Refreshing, hell," Henry Firth said. "I don't care how disingenuous this young man is. If I have to charge him with something, he'll start singing a different tune—how whatever he said is inadmissible because he was deprived of counsel."

"Are you thinking of charging him?" Cora said. "Believe me, Minami will be relieved."

Judge Hobbs banged the gavel. "That will do. Everyone is aware that there are two parties involved. We do not need to be constantly reminded. If this young man wants to testify, swear him in."

Dennis took the oath.

Cora said, "Dennis, I know this is a ticklish situation. I'm not going to ask anything that might get you into trouble. Let's start with a few preliminaries. You were being blackmailed by Thelma Wilson?"

Henry Firth jumped to his feet. "Objection! After that fine speech about this young man not needing representation, she comes out and accuses him of a crime!"

"I don't think *being* blackmailed is a crime, Your Honor. *Blackmail* is, but no one's charging Thelma Wilson."

"Nonetheless, Miss Felton, you are treading a very fine line."

"Might I point out that the witness hasn't answered the question?"

"I haven't ruled on the objection."

"That's probably why, Your Honor."

A ripple of amusement ran through the crowd. Once again, Judge Hobbs wondered what he could possibly do that would not make him seem more foolish.

"I want to answer, Your Honor," Dennis said. "Only my attorney has advised me not to."

"Your attorney?"

"Becky Baldwin."

"Ms. Baldwin, have you so advised your client?"

"Yes, Your Honor."

"Well, there you are. We have a clear-cut conflict of interest. It is obviously in your other client's best interests to have him answer."

"I fail to see why, Your Honor."

"You fail to see *why*?"

"With all due respect, Your Honor—"

"Excuse me," Cora said, "but I believe I am speaking in Ms.

Baldwin's behalf. I would like to point out that as attorney in this case, Ms. Baldwin is privy to some facts to which you, the judge, are not. And to which the prosecutor is not. I would like to point out that that is right and proper, and within the scope of a defense attorney. She is under no obligation to make any of this information available to anyone. In fact, during the course of the trial, she is not obliged to put on any evidence whatsoever but may merely attack the prosecutor's side of the case. And many defenses have been waged and won on that notion. If, however, she is astute enough to realize that her client's case cannot be compromised by the withholding of evidence that is irrelevant to the situation, there can be no conflict to resolve."

"Once again," Henry Firth said, "the woman is making an assertion that is unsupported by facts. I defy her to produce any evidence to back up this wild assertion."

"Miss Felton," Judge Hobbs said, "I understand your contention. But your argument is unconvincing. I am still waiting to hear something of substance."

"Very well," Cora said, "call Minami."

The Sudoku Lady rose from her seat next to Becky Baldwin, and in full geisha garb trailing clouds of silk, paraded to the witness stand.

"You are calling the defendant?" Judge Hobbs said, incredulously.

"I have no objection, Your Honor," Henry Firth put in brightly.

"I'm sure you don't. But her attorney should object. Ms. Baldwin. You are this woman's attorney?"

Becky smiled. "That is what this hearing is to determine."

"But you *claim* to be her attorney?"

"I *am* her attorney. Unless you rule otherwise."

"And you are allowing her to take the stand?"

"Absolutely, Your Honor."

"She will not only be questioned by Cora Felton but she will also be interrogated by the district attorney. Who, no doubt, will give her a rigorous interrogation."

"I'm sure he will, Your Honor. And I'm sure it won't hurt her in the least. My client is innocent and has nothing to hide."

"If she has nothing to hide, why won't you let her tell her story?" Henry Firth blurted out.

"Oh, Your Honor," Cora Felton said, "I assign that remark as a blatant attempt to castigate the defendant for exercising her constitutional rights."

"I fear it is," Judge Hobbs said. "Though I appreciate the frustration from which it sprang. Mr. Firth, if you could attempt to control your temper."

"Yes, Your Honor."

"Ms. Baldwin. Before we proceed further, let me make one more attempt to clarify the situation. You do understand that should your client reveal something that was damaging to her in the course of this examination, the only grounds on which she could argue for it being inadmissible during the trial, would be that she was inadequately represented by an incompetent attorney, whose ineptitude was so great as to constitute legal malpractice."

"Well put, Your Honor," Cora said. "Becky, did you hear that? If you mess up, the only way she gets off is proving you're a dummy. Is that okay with you?"

Becky smiled. "This may surprise you, but I understood the situation even without your interpretation. Your Honor, I am concerned for neither my client's safety nor my own. May we continue?"

Judge Hobbs scowled. "One moment. Should it turn out that you have jeopardized your client's safety in an effort not to *lose* your client, that would not be taken lightly."

Cora smiled. "I think no one could claim she has not been duly warned, Your Honor."

"Very well. As long as that is understood, you may proceed."

"Thank you, Your Honor. Minami, you are known in Japan as the Sudoku Lady?"

"Yes, I am."

"Just as I am known as the Puzzle Lady over here?"

"Yes."

"Tell me something. When sudoku are found at crime scenes in Japan, do the police consider you a suspect?"

Minami smiled. "They do not. They ask for my help. In my own country I have actually assisted the police in solving several crimes."

"So you don't feel the presence of sudoku puzzles at crime scenes should reflect adversely on you?"

"I beg your pardon?"

"I'm sorry. There were sudoku at the crime scenes. That doesn't mean you're guilty."

"Of course not. What a silly idea."

"You think it's silly that the police consider you a suspect?"

"Of course it is. I didn't kill anyone."

"Oh, Your Honor," Henry Firth said, "this is not testimony. This is just a self-serving declaration. I'm sure if we let her, this woman could go on proclaiming her innocence all afternoon. Her bland assurance is not evidence. Any more than her attorney's assurance that her legal rights are not being compromised."

"I quite agree," Judge Hobbs said. "Miss Felton, we take your point. Could you move things along?"

"Yes, Your Honor. Minami, you know that Dennis Pride received a blackmail letter from Thelma Wilson?"

"I don't know it for a fact. I heard you say so."

"Exactly. Tell me, did Thelma Wilson send *you* a blackmail letter?"

The question produced an uproar in the courtroom.

Judge Hobbs banged the gavel. "Order! Order in the court! Miss Felton, were you an attorney, I would assign that question as misconduct, betraying the rights of the client you were sworn to protect. As you are a layperson speaking for Becky Baldwin, such is not the case. Nonetheless, I would expect the woman's attorney to object."

"I have no objection," Becky said.

"And I certainly have no objection," Henry Firth added.

"Well, *someone* should object," Judge Hobbs said. "The woman is the defendant in a murder case. The question is highly detrimental to her well-being, establishing a clear-cut motive for the crime."

"Oh, pooh," Cora said, "she has a motive for the murder, Your Honor. Everyone knows that. We'll stipulate to it."

Judge Hobbs's eyes were bugging out of his head. "*You* can't stipulate to it! You're not an *attorney*!"

"Well, they make you go to law school," Cora said. "I'm sick of school."

"Miss Felton, this is no laughing matter. You're not an attorney, but you can be held in contempt of court. I've warned you before, and I'm warning you again. Have some respect for the courtroom."

"Yes, Your Honor. But if we're going to clear up this minor matter of whether these clients can share representation, we have to examine the facts. And the fact is, this woman got a blackmail note. If you'd rather have her attorney stipulate to it, I understand."

Becky stood up. "I'm willing to stipulate to the note, Your Honor."

Judge Hobbs glowered. "You realize you're just digging yourself in deeper."

Becky smiled. "Not at all, Your Honor. The facts of the case exonerate me, just as they do my client. I know it perfectly well, and, if we're allowed to advance them, you'll know it, too."

"Now *you're* bordering on contempt of court."

"I'm sorry. No disrespect meant, Your Honor, but it's hard to establish your innocence when people keep telling you not to."

"You claim this blackmail note demonstrates your client's innocence?"

"Only incidentally, Your Honor. With regard to the matter at hand, it demonstrates why I should be free to act as her attorney. I would like to reiterate that I have been duly warned about my responsibilities to my client and myself and that I know what I am doing. So, if you'll allow Miss Felton to continue, I think you'll be satisfied with the results."

"If I may continue, Your Honor," Cora said, "we just established this woman got a blackmail note. I would imagine everyone would like to know something about it. What do you say we find out?"

Without waiting for the judge to rule, Cora turned back to Minami. "In what form was this blackmail note?"

"It was a crossword puzzle and a sudoku."

The place went wild.

Chapter

4 9

Judge Hobbs nearly broke his gavel, but he finally got the court-room quieted. "All right, that will do," he said. "Another outburst of this type, and I will clear the courtroom. The only reason I'm not doing it now is I appreciate the rather spectacular nature of what you just heard. However, the element of surprise is over. Should this happen again, I will clear the court. Miss Felton, you may proceed. I just hope you know what you are doing."

"You and me both, Your Honor," Cora said. "Minami, you just testified you got a blackmail note in the form of a crossword puzzle and a sudoku. How did you get it?"

"It was delivered to my motel."

"Were you there at the time?"

"No, I was in jail. My niece brought it to me."

"Did your niece see who delivered it?"

"No. It was in an envelope slipped under the door."

"Was there anything else in the envelope?"

"No. Just the crossword puzzle and the sudoku."

"What did it say on the envelope?"

"'To the Sudoku Lady.'"

"Was there a return address?"

"No."

"How did you know it was a blackmail note?"

"The crossword puzzle said so."

"What did it say?"

"'Sit in jail for a spell. Never fear, I won't tell.'"

"Who was it from?"

"Thelma Wilson."

"But you say it wasn't signed. How could you tell?"

"There were clues in the puzzle."

"Oh?"

"Yes. They referred to the sudoku. They told me which numbers to choose."

"Could you explain that to the court?"

"Yes. Clue 17 Across was 'Horizontal row in sudoku.' The answer was 'Fifth.' That told me to look at the fifth row across.

"Clue 29 Across was 'Number of numbers in numbered row.' The answer was 'Three.' That told me to look at the first three numbers in row five.

"28 Down was 'With sudoku, address of house you went in.' The answer was 'Elm.'

"With the three numbers from the sudoku, the answer was '146 Elm.'"

"And what did 146 Elm mean to you?"

"It did not mean anything to me. I had to have my niece look it up."

"What did she find?"

"146 Elm was the address of Sheila Preston."

"The woman who was killed?"

"Yes."

"The woman who lived across the street from Thelma Wilson?"

"Yes."

"And Sheila Preston was the woman you were in jail on suspicion of murdering?"

"That's right."

"So, the sudoku that came with the crossword puzzle turned out to mean something?"

"Yes, it did."

"How about the sudoku found on the body of Sheila Preston? Did that mean anything?"

"No, it did not."

"And the sudoku found with Thelma Wilson. What about that one?"

"It did not mean anything either."

"When the police let you go, did they know about the puzzle and the sudoku your niece found at the motel?"

"No, they did not."

"But you did, and you knew what they meant?"

"Yes, I did."

"So, when you got out of jail, did you immediately go kill Thelma Wilson?"

"No, I did not."

"What did you do?"

"I went to see you."

"But not to kill me?"

"No."

"Why did you come to see me?"

"To tell you I was out of jail. And that the contest could continue."

"What contest?"

"To see who could solve the crime."

"And why should we do that?"

"Because that is what I do in my country. And that is what you do in yours."

"I see," Cora said. "So you came here to challenge me, is that right?"

Minami nodded. "Yes."

Cora unbuttoned her long tweed coat, took it off, and threw it on the defense table. She was wearing a white *gi*, the Japanese martial arts uniform. She pivoted on Minami and struck a karate pose.

"Bring it on!"

Chapter

5 0

Judge Hobbs was livid. "Miss Felton! That will do! I warned you about such demonstrations in my courtroom!"

"Well, I wish you'd make up your mind," Cora said. "If you recall, you ordered me to take my coat off. I'm only trying to please."

"I doubt that very much," Judge Hobbs said dryly. "You clearly planned this theatrical demonstration. You had better have a good reason why."

"Oh, but I do, Your Honor. It goes to the crux of the case. Minami came here to meet me. Why? She said so herself. To take me on. A little friendly competition. The battle of the century. The Sudoku Lady versus the Puzzle Lady. That's what this is all about.

"You see, my sudoku books are sold in Japan. It happened that on one particular week, one of my books outsold one of hers.

Why, I couldn't begin to tell you. But probably because I'm new. I'm a novelty. I'm an American. I'm different. Whatever the reason, it happened, and that's why she's here. To drum up some business for her first American release. And, by meeting me, create some publicity for her own series back home. I don't think she ever dreamed how much publicity she was actually going to get. The book isn't even out yet, and it's already in the top hundred on Amazon.com. Which would be another motive for the murder. She killed these people to boost her sales. And if you buy that, I have this land in Florida."

Cora turned back to the witness. "Minami, you investigated the death of Ida Fielding and concluded it was a murder, did you not?"

"Yes, I did."

"Based on what evidence?"

"Just a minute," Judge Hobbs said. "Despite the fact no one is objecting, I can't sit idly by. You're now asking her to incriminate herself in the crime."

"Not at all, Your Honor. She isn't even charged with that murder. Which, in my humble opinion, was never a murder to begin with. However, since you raise the point, Mr. Firth, do you have any intention whatsoever of charging Minami with that crime?"

"I don't have to answer to you."

"No, you don't. You're an elected official. You have to answer to the people. I see a bunch of 'em here. You guys wanna know what really happened?"

"Oh, Your Honor," Henry Firth said, "that is clearly improper. Just because she isn't a lawyer doesn't mean she doesn't have to follow legal procedure."

"Exactly," Judge Hobbs said. "Miss Felton, I'm not going to warn you again."

"I'm glad to hear it, Your Honor. It *is* getting annoying."

Judge Hobbs banged the gavel. "And that flippant remark will cost you fifty dollars. Do I make myself clear?"

"Absolutely, Your Honor. I humbly apologize. But I hope *my* point is well taken. I'm asking Minami about the death of Ida Fielding. Which she has not been charged with and which has not even been ruled a homicide. I would point out that the minute I started that line of questioning, Your Honor said it was not proper because she was a defendant. Suppose I asked her about the Lindbergh kidnapping, for instance. Would you say she can't answer because she's a defendant?"

Judge Hobbs seemed torn between upping the fine to a hundred and answering the question. "You may proceed. But tread lightly, and try not to be facetious."

"Yes, Your Honor." Cora turned back to Minami. "What evidence did you find?"

"I found evidence the two husbands appeared to have been involved with each other's wives."

"Did that make you think of *Strangers on a Train*? Referring to an old Alfred Hitchcock film where two men kill each other's wives. I was wondering if you thought that happened here?"

"No, I do not."

"There," Cora said. "Was there ever a clearer indication of innocence? The defendant rejects out of hand the suggestion the killer was someone other than herself."

"I find that less than persuasive," Henry Firth said.

"I find this whole line of argument less than persuasive," Judge Hobbs ruled. "We have one pseudo-lawyer in karate clothes questioning a defendant who should not be on the stand to begin with. Is it your hope, Miss Felton, that if you make sufficient mockery of the case, the prosecutor will give in and allow Ms. Baldwin to act as her own attorney?"

"That would be nice, Your Honor. But while we're here, I'd rather clear the whole thing up."

"I beg your pardon?"

"I mean the murders. Or should I say *murder* because, basically, we only have one murder here."

"How can you say that?"

"I've been authorized as amicus curiae to speak in the attorney's behalf."

"That's not what I mean and you know it. The defendant is charged with two murders. What makes you think you can summarily dismiss one?"

"See, that's the problem," Cora said, "you're talking about two murder charges. But we have three dead women. Any self-respecting serial killer would have done them all. And if the Sudoku Lady is anything, she is not haphazard."

"You're unhappy she's not charged with all three murders?"

"Heaven's no. I'm unhappy she's charged with any. Because you really can't have a decent serial killer if someone's doing his or her work. When I read that in a murder mystery, I throw it across the room. It's almost as bad as a convoluted courtroom scene where the amateur detective gets away with all kinds of stuff that would never be admissible in a real courtroom."

Judge Hobbs was too stupefied to come up with a reprimand. He sat on the bench with his mouth hanging open.

"Anyway, that's where you make your big mistake. You think there are three murders, you charge her with two, and then what? After that, nothing's going to work. Three murders is all wrong.

The way I see it, you've got one accident, one murder, and one case of self-defense."

"Objection! Counsel is making a speech and stating facts not in evidence."

"Exactly," Judge Hobbs said.

"Then let's get them in evidence," Cora said. "If I could withdraw the witness briefly, I can lay the proper groundwork."

"Objection," Henry Firth said. "This woman is not leaving the stand until I have a chance to cross-examine her."

"You'll get your chance," Cora said. "But when you do, you might as well have some facts to play with. You just objected that they're not in evidence. Are you telling me you object if they are?"

Henry Firth looked as befuddled as the judge.

"So, with your permission, I'd like to withdraw the witness." Cora put up her hand. "Temporarily. She's still in your crosshairs. Just long enough to clear up the minor matter of how many crimes we have."

"Oh, let her do it," Judge Hobbs said. "It will take less time than arguing. The witness may step down. Who do you wish to call?"

"Call Irving Swartzman."

"Who?" Henry Firth said.

"Her agent."

"Her *literary* agent?"

"Her *American* literary agent. I assume her Japanese one is in Japan."

"What do you expect to prove by him?"

"I told you. How many crimes we're talking about."

"How would her literary agent know that?"

"I never said he did. But I need to lay the groundwork to explain my theory."

Henry Firth raised his hands. "Whoa! Whoa! You said you were going to introduce some facts. Not lay the groundwork for some absurd flight of fancy. Do you mean this man is just one of *several* witnesses you intend to call?"

"I may need to call others," Cora admitted.

"Your Honor," Henry Firth sputtered, "you see what is happening here? She's taken the defendant off the stand. Now, in the guise of presenting facts, she's going to call witness after witness to testify to some nebulous theory, just so I can never cross-examine."

"Oh, pooh," Cora said, "I could finish with the witnesses in the time it takes to handle your objections. If anyone is postponing your cross-examination, it's you."

"Your Honor, who's ruling on my objection, you or her?"

"I am," Judge Hobbs said, "but her point is well taken. We're spending all our time arguing procedure. Let's hear what the witness has to say. If you don't like it, you can object to the questions and I'll rule on your objections. But I would advise you not to be overly technical because it will not speed things along. Mr. Swartzman, take the stand."

The flamboyant agent seemed eager to testify. He raised his hand, took the oath, and preened in front of the TV cameras.

"Your name is Irving Swartzman, you are Minami, the Sudoku Lady's American agent?"

"That's right."

"You just heard her on the stand. Do you have any problem with what she said?"

He seemed surprised by the question. "Of course not."

"Mr. Swartzman, how many crimes do you think there are?"

"I don't understand the question."

"It's what we've been talking about. Of the three women's deaths, how many of them were murder?"

"I don't know. I suppose they all are."

"You haven't given it much thought?"

"No, I haven't."

"That's surprising, since your client's been charged with them. Of course, that hasn't been bad for you, has it?"

"I beg your pardon?"

"The publicity's put her on the best-seller list. It couldn't be more convenient had you planned it."

"Well, I assure you I didn't."

"No, I don't think you did either. But it certainly was a lucky break."

"It's rather callous to think of it that way."

"Yes, it is. But I can't help it. As a result of your client's being charged with murder, she's surged past me on Amazon.com. And her book's not even out yet."

"You're jealous of my client?" Swartzman said incredulously.

"Absolutely. She's younger, thinner, prettier, and she's Asian to boot. If I were her, life would be one big party."

Swartzman smirked. "I'm sure it would. I was referring to her sales figures."

"Of course you were. That's your job. That's why you got her here in the first place. I'm right about that, aren't I? You're responsible for her coming here and meeting me. That was to publicize a book."

"That's my job."

"Yes, it is. And you do it well. Only this time you tried to do it *too* well. You overstepped, and that's what started this whole mess."

"Do I hear a question?" Henry Firth said.

"Sorry. I'll make it a question. Isn't it a fact the whole idea of challenging me to solve Ida Fielding's death came from you?"

"I may have suggested it."

"I thought you might have. It seemed a harmless idea at first. The Puzzle Lady versus the Sudoku Lady. A friendly wager, perhaps some play in the press. Only you pushed a little too hard. I can't believe a clever woman like Minami would have taken the Ida Fielding death for a murder. Because it clearly was an accidental death. Without any prodding or meddling or friendly wagers, it gets chalked up for what it was, an accident, and that's the end of it. But that wouldn't sell any books. So you encouraged Minami to keep it alive."

Swartzman smiled. "How do you know it *wasn't* a murder?"

"Are you accusing Minami of that crime, too?"

"Of course not. My client didn't kill anyone. As the evidence will show."

"I certainly hope so. Still, I find it strange, you pushing for murder under the circumstances. But let's move on. The second death is much more illuminating. First, because it's second. That sounds silly, doesn't it? But it happens to be the case. The most telling thing about Sheila Preston's death is that it happens to be the second time. Two accidents inside of a week? I don't think so. Not to two women who might or might not have been involved with each other's husbands, yada, yada, yada. No, this is clearly something else, and as if there was any doubt, a sudoku was left at the scene. What do you make of that, Mr. Swartzman?"

"It's exactly what it seems like. Someone is trying to frame Minami for the crime."

"That would be handy, wouldn't it? If the sudoku suggested a frame. That would be the best of all possible worlds. The Sudoku Lady would be involved without any peril to herself. Unfortunately, the police and prosecution took the sudoku at face value, and arrested Minami for the murder."

"Which is utterly ridiculous."

"Granted. But, my, what publicity. You couldn't have asked for anything better, could you?"

"Believe me, it's not what I wanted."

"Really? An incredible spike in sales? My agent takes a percentage of my earnings. Are you telling me you do it for love? That jump in sales benefits you enormously. If you bring the woman here from Japan at great expense and her book tanks, everyone's blaming you. But if sales go through the roof, you're a miracle worker, a super-agent, a go-to guy."

Swartzman smiled. "I'm afraid that's out of my control."

"Is it really? After the showdown at the police station where Minami failed to prove a crime, you took it on yourself to repair the damage, to do something about it, to make her look good. Because that, of course, was the whole point. You yourself started investigating, pushing for anything that could help your client. You laid the groundwork for a story of infidelity and betrayal and backstabbing. I bet if we dug deep enough, we'd find that all of the rumors about the alleged affairs between the various husbands and wives could be traced at least indirectly back to you."

"That's absurd."

"Is it? I bet you spoke to a lot of people. So far, no one's commented on it because it's peripheral and unimportant, but I'm willing to bet you approached the parties involved. Or are you telling me you never spoke to either of the husbands, Jason Fielding or Steve Preston?"

"Of course I talked to them. It's only natural that I would. After all, my client's been accused—"

"Yes, yes, yes," Cora said, holding up her hand. "But I bet if we pinned it down, we'd find you spoke to them even *before* her arrest."

"What's your point?"

"*Did* you speak to them before her arrest?"

"She was arrested twice."

"Her first arrest."

"With so much happening, how could I possibly remember?"

Cora nodded approvingly. "Good tack to take. A denial could be a disaster, if it turned out to be wrong." She grimaced. "Even so, it's a problem. See, you're allowing for the fact you might have been questioning people before Minami went to jail. If you didn't do it, you don't have to allow for it. There's no how-can-I-remember about it. You can remember very easily. Her being arrested was what set you off. See what I mean?"

"Finally, a question!" Henry Firth said. "Your Honor, is she going to be allowed to make these speeches?"

"If that's an objection, it's overruled," Judge Hobbs said. "I'm interested in this line of questioning. The witness may answer."

Swartzman smiled. "I'm sorry, but I don't recall the question."

"The question is simple," Cora said. "How is it possible you can't remember whether it was before or after Minami was arrested for the first time when you questioned people? You either had a reason to do so *before* her arrest or you didn't."

"Well—"

"Well, what?"

"I was interested."

"Are you saying you did?"

"I'm saying I might have. I was promoting the idea. I was frustrated by the fact it wasn't going anywhere. I made up my *mind* to look into it. See what I mean? And I *did* look into it. But whether she was arrested before or after I began to look into it, I'm not sure. The sequence of events is the only thing confusing me. And after all that's happened, that's only natural."

"It's only natural, but it's not convincing. It sounds like the type of justification a person thinks up because they have to. Because they have to justify a lie. So why would you lie? You may not have killed Sheila Preston. Let's say you didn't. That suits me—I don't even think it's a murder. So let's say you didn't. Then why would you lie? Why wouldn't you tell the absolute truth? Why would you need to cover your tracks with vague, unconvincing statements about having decided to question people but not remembering when you started to do so? If you talked to Sheila Preston, you'd know whether it was before or after Minami was arrested. Because Minami was arrested for killing Sheila Preston. And you may be a great agent, but I doubt if you can interview the dead. So, let me ask you point-blank—did you talk to Sheila Preston?"

"No, I did not."

"Of course not. Because, if you had, you would know for a fact it was before Minami was arrested. But if you never spoke to Sheila Preston, why would you feel guilty enough to hedge your bets about when you began talking to people about the crime? Is there anything with regard to this case you might not wish to admit?"

Cora held up one finger. "Yes, there is.

"The sudoku.

"The sudoku found with the body. Which resulted in Minami getting arrested and precipitated this entire situation. I put it to you, Mr. Swartzman, if you began questioning the witnesses in this case and got to Sheila Preston and walked in and found her dead, well, a lot of things might have occurred to you. The first is, this proved the Sudoku Lady right. She said it was a murder, and it *was* a murder. The second death proved it. Unless you believe in coincidences, there was no other explanation.

"However, Minami had just been at the police station, where

her ideas were totally undermined. She had lost favor with the police, who would be much more inclined to listen to me, the Puzzle Lady, local girl who has been right in the past, than some upstart foreigner who has already been proven wrong.

"How could you ensure the fact Minami would be taken seriously? Simple. You were carrying samples of her work. You merely leave one with the body. A sudoku with the corpse and it's a natural the Sudoku Lady will be called in to solve the crime. What you didn't count on was her being accused of it."

"I assure you, I did nothing of the sort." Swartzman sneered.

"No? I can see why you wouldn't want to admit it in front of your client, considering the position she's in. But it's really not your fault. The sudoku wouldn't have implicated her if she hadn't called on the decedent. Thelma Wilson saw her go in. Thelma Wilson saw her come out. Minami had a lot of poise, but I doubt if she's as good as you are at hiding the fact she just saw a corpse. She found the body, saw the sudoku lying next to it, freaked out, and ran.

"You can't really blame her. She was afraid to call the police under the circumstances, for fear they would think exactly what they did. She had to report the crime, but she wanted to find the body in the presence of a witness. She ran and got her niece and came back. Unfortunately, she was too late. The police caught her there, and Thelma Wilson volunteered the information that it was her second visit, and that's all she wrote.

"So, why did the killer leave a sudoku on the body of Thelma Wilson? Copycat. Not copycat crime, copycat *puzzle*. If the sudoku implicates the Sudoku Lady, wonderful. Let's implicate her again. The killer doesn't want to be caught for the crime. The killer's perfectly happy to have a fall guy." Cora grimaced. "I suppose I should say fall person. I just get fed up with these PC terms.

"Anyway, Minami's released from jail, and lo and behold, what should turn up but another body with a sudoku attached. Naturally, the police arrest her again, and there she sits.

"The question now is who killed Thelma Wilson? It wasn't Minami, for no matter how inclined the police might be to take the evidence at face value, there is no way the woman is so colossally stupid as to commit another murder the minute she gets out of jail and, just in case the police didn't think to suspect her, leave a sudoku along with it. Not possible, didn't happen. The Sudoku Lady is innocent. We have to look somewhere else.

"And here we have no lack of suspects. As I've already pointed out, Dennis Pride is a prime example. Thelma Wilson tried to blackmail him for going into Sheila Preston's house. I know, I know, I haven't been allowed to introduce it into evidence because his lawyer won't let him talk, and his lawyer is also her lawyer, and that's why we're here. But just for the sake of argument, let's say he was in Sheila Preston's house and got a blackmail note. And just for the sake of argument, let's say *you* were in Sheila Preston's house. You'd have to have been to leave the sudoku. And if Thelma Wilson saw you there, *you'd* get a blackmail note. Isn't that what happened?"

"Most certainly not."

"'Most *certainly* not'? That's a rather vehement denial. 'No' would suffice. But that isn't enough for you. You're absolutely *certain*. Forgive me for saying so, but that's the type of finality that leads one to think there *is* doubt.

"So, say you got a blackmail note. You'd be in a position of having to confront Thelma Wilson. And if she accused you of killing Sheila Preston, you might have to kill her."

"That's ridiculous. I didn't kill Sheila Preston."

"I never said you did. I said if she *accused* you of it. Thelma

Wilson made a lot of accusations. The woman was like Babe Ruth. She hit home runs, but she struck out a lot, too. So, if she accused you of something you hadn't done, but it might look like you had, she would put you in a very bad position. You might have to kill her."

"You're crazy."

"Even though it would hurt your client. You might have to kill her and leave the sudoku."

"I did nothing of the sort!"

"The police found your fingerprints on the sudoku."

"Impossible! I didn't leave that sudoku!"

Cora's head snapped up. "You didn't leave *that* sudoku? Are you telling me you left the other sudoku?"

"No. I didn't leave any sudoku."

"Then why did you specify that one?"

"Because that was the one you were talking about."

Cora shook her head. "Nice cover, but it doesn't fly. Your first reaction was, 'Oh, my God, the police must have mixed up the sudoku. They must be talking about the one I left at Sheila's house.'"

"No, it wasn't. I didn't do it."

"Oh, no? I explained it's a perfectly innocent action on your part. Drumming up some publicity for your client. But I can see why you wouldn't want to admit leaving it, because that would make it look like you left the second one, which would make it look like you killed Thelma Wilson. Which we know you didn't do."

Swartzman, in mid-denial, stopped, let out his breath in a sigh. He blinked twice. "Then what are you getting at?"

Cora grinned. "Felt good, didn't it? To hear yourself cleared of the one thing you'd been afraid of. The only crime you actually did. Because that's all you're guilty of. Killing Thelma Wilson, who tried to blackmail you for the crime you *didn't* do. Killing

Sheila Preston. Which wasn't a murder at all but a case of self-defense."

Henry Firth was on his feet. "Oh, Your Honor—"

Judge Hobbs cut him off in mid-objection. "Silence. Whatever you're about to say is overruled. Miss Felton, can you put that in the form of a question?"

Cora frowned. "Funny. You don't look like Alex Trebek. But I'll give it a shot. Mr. Swartzman, is it or is it not true that you killed Sheila Preston in legitimate self-defense? You called on her and tried to enlist her aid in bolstering the stories you were spreading. She was enraged to find you were telling lies about her husband and her poor, dead friend. She flew at you in a blind fury. Which effectively made her murder self-defense. If you'd called the cops, you might have made that stick. Only you couldn't afford to. Even if you beat the rap, it would have killed your career when it came out what you were up to. So you took lemons and made lemonade. If the police were going to think it was a murder, it might as well be a *useful* murder. You left the sudoku, got the hell out of there, and the rest is history."

Cora smiled. "I'm sorry. That was supposed to be in the form of a question, so I'll ask one." She cocked her head at the agent. "Don't you feel stupid now?"

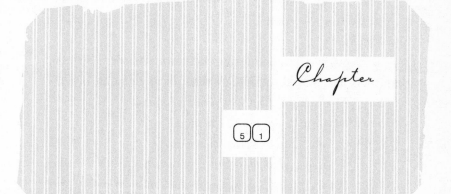

Chapter

5 1

Chief Harper came in the door of his office to find Cora Felton waiting for him.

"Oh. You're here."

"You don't sound pleased."

"It's been a long day."

"Well, I had to find out what happened."

"You know what happened. You exposed Minami's agent as the killer and made me look like a fool."

"I'm sorry you feel that way. But, trust me, Chief, you didn't come off half as bad as Judge Hobbs and Ratface."

"I told you not to call him that."

"Why not? He's a judge."

"Cora."

"The case is over, Chief. It's good news for everyone. You're the arresting officer—you get the credit."

"But you figured it out."

"That's what I do. And I only have to because we have such diabolically clever killers in this town. The average killer shoots his wife because she pisses him off. I'm sure you'd have no trouble solving that."

"Thanks a lot." Chief Harper flopped down in his desk chair and glared at Cora. "Would you take off that ridiculous karate outfit?"

"Why, Chief Harper! And you, a married man."

"Don't kid around. I'm not in the mood."

"So, let's have it. Did Swartzman confess?"

Harper shook his head. "Clammed up and asked for a lawyer. Bit of a problem. Becky Baldwin wouldn't take the case. Something about a conflict of interest."

"Oh, well, we wouldn't want that."

"He called someone in New York, but it's gonna take the guy a while to get here."

"Tough break."

"Yeah."

"What about Minami?"

"Becky's bailing her out. Her niece is waiting to pick her up." Harper's eyes narrowed. "Was she in on your charade?"

"Why, Chief Harper, you see conspiracies everywhere."

"Yeah."

"You need any help breaking Swartzman?"

"I don't think so. Since your little stunt, people have been coming forward. There's a whole bunch can attest to Swartzman creeping around poking his nose in. Dan's taking witness statements now. All in all, Henry Firth's pretty damn happy."

"I live to make his day."

Sherry Carter and Becky Baldwin came in, giggling like school-girls. It was the friendliest Cora had seen them together since Sherry married Becky's old boyfriend.

"Hey, kids," Cora said, "what's so funny?"

"Minami's a free woman," Sherry said.

"So?"

"So," Becky said, "she no longer requires my services. Which effectively resolves the conflict of interest. I am now completely free to represent Dennis Pride. I began by advising the son of a bitch to get the hell out of town before someone arrests him for violating his restraining order."

"She did," Sherry said, "and before he could argue with her, I showed up and he had to leave. As long as Becky and I stick together, he has to stay a hundred yards away from her."

"But he still has to pay me," Becky said. "I really like the arrangement."

The door burst open and a cloud of silk swept in, with a teenager in tow.

"Ah, Miss Felton!" Minami cried, "I am so glad you are here. I can't thank you enough."

"Don't sweat it. It was fun, wasn't it?"

Minami's eyes gleamed. "Yes, it was. I have solved crimes, but you do the spectacular. You stage events. It is exciting."

"Oh, no," Michiko said, "now look what you've done. There will be no holding her back. I know her. She is going to do the same thing when we get home."

"What's wrong with that?" Cora said. "You have to let the old girl have some fun."

"Old? I am not old."

"Of course not. Well, maybe compared to me. But you are still young at heart."

Minami looked at her. "You joke. I do not mind. Today you can do whatever you want. I am free again and everything is all right."

"Of course, you may need a new agent."

"I may. But that should not be hard to find. The book is doing well."

"Now there's an understatement."

"You must come to Japan. Perhaps we could solve a crime together there."

"I don't know," Cora said. "My Japanese is not as good as your English."

"You know Japanese?"

"A little. Toyota. Mitsubishi."

"I could translate for you," Michiko said.

"That's all I need," Cora said. "A teenage interpreter. I'll wind up getting tattooed at a Japanese rock concert."

"I would not do that," Michiko said.

"No, but *she* would." Sherry smiled. "Don't trust her, Minami. The woman is a bad influence."

"I thank you for the warning." Minami bowed to Cora. "Still, you are welcome."

"Sure, now that I saved you from a murder rap. Tomorrow it will be, 'What have you done for me lately?' "

"That depends."

"On what?"

Minami smiled. "The best-seller list."

Chapter

5 2

"Well, that worked out," Sherry said as they drove home.

"Yes, I think so," Cora said. "Even when you figure in the price of a karate outfit. Can I take it off my taxes as publicity?"

"Ask your agent. At least he's not in jail."

"No, he's not." Cora frowned. "I bet my books would sell better if he was."

"Cora."

"Just a thought. I'm not framing the son of a bitch."

"Why is he a son of a bitch? He's done very well by you."

"I still haven't forgiven him for booking me into that Granville Grains publicity tour."

"Hey, don't knock publicity. Publicity sells books."

"Well, it did for Minami."

"Yeah." Sherry took a breath. "So. About you moving out—"

"I'll get to it," Cora said irritably. "I've been a little busy."

"I'm not trying to rush you. But you're right about the house not being big enough."

"That's all I'm saying."

"I spoke to Aaron, and he agrees, and he wanted me to talk to you before we got home. Because he had to go back to the paper to write the story."

"There's nothing to talk about. It was my idea."

"Yeah, but he didn't want you to freak out."

"Why would I freak out?"

"About the backhoe."

"Huh?"

"The backhoe in the driveway. And the builders staking out the ground."

"What?"

"You're right. The house is too small. So we're adding on: three bedrooms, two baths, game room in the basement."

"Basement?"

"Yeah. It's two stories with a basement. You can have your own pool table. Aaron figured it would keep you out of mischief. I know better, but take the table. It's one of the perks."

Cora's mouth was open. She blinked. "Sherry. Is that true?"

"More or less. The backhoe's not there yet. Or the builders. They start next week."

Cora shook her head. "I can't believe it. Why are you doing this?"

"How many times have you been divorced and you have to ask me that? You got married, things changed, you didn't like it. Aaron and I are very happy. We got married. If that means throwing you out, we'll start to resent it. Better we start to resent *you*."

"You already resent me."

"See? It's working."

"But how can you afford it? This is a hell of a time to finance a house."

"Well, it turns out your sudoku books are doing so well, you just sold a whole new line of crossword puzzle books."

"I did?"

"You sure did. Which would be a real chore if you had to write them, but since all you have to do is pose for a picture or two, I didn't feel that guilty saying yes."

"Oh, my God." Cora was utterly overwhelmed. She opened her mouth, closed it again. "I don't know what to say."

"Now, there's a first." Sherry grinned and breezily changed the subject. "So, how'd you get Minami to cooperate? She can't have felt too kindly toward you. Before you got her off, I mean."

"Easy. I knew her secret. She doesn't write sudoku. Her niece does it for her."

"You blackmailed her?" Sherry said. She frowned. "No, that can't be it. She was positively cordial to you just now."

"Well, I won her confidence."

"How?"

"I shared a secret with her."

Sherry's eyes widened. "Oh, my God! You told her I write your crossword puzzles! You said, 'What a coincidence. Your niece writes your puzzles and my niece writes mine.' No wonder you're thick as thieves. That's it, isn't it?"

"Are you kidding me?" Cora countered. "Trust her with a secret like that? Come on. She's not family."

"So what did you tell her?"

"Told her I left the sudoku." Cora shrugged. "I figured that was a big enough secret. I said, 'Hey, babe, I framed you for murder. How you like them apples?'"